Enid Blyton's

MR STAMP-ABOUT IN A FIX

and other stories

D1638886

CLIVEDEN PRESS

Published in Great Britain in 1992 by Cliveden Press,
an Egmont Company, Egmont House, PO Box 111,
Great Ducie Street, Manchester M60 3BL.
Printed in the United Kingdom.

ISBN 0 7498 1228 1

Enid Blyton

Enid Blyton was born in London in 1897. Her childhood was spent in Beckenham, Kent, and as a child she began to write poems, stories and plays. She trained to be a teacher but she devoted her whole life to being a children's author. Her first book was a collection of poems for children, published in 1922. In 1926 she began to write a weekly magazine for children called *Sunny Stories*, and it was here that many of her most popular stories and characters first appeared. The magazine was immensely popular and in 1953 it became *The Enid Blyton Magazine*.

She wrote more than 600 books for children and many of her most popular series are still published all over the world. Her books have been translated into over 30 languages. Enid Blyton died in 1968.

Contents

Millicent Mary's surprise

Once there was a little girl called Millicent Mary. She had a dear little garden of her own, and in the early spring the very first things that came up were the white snowdrops.

Millicent Mary loved them. She loved the straight green stalks that came up, holding the white bud tightly wrapped up at the top. She liked the two green leaves that sprang up each side. She loved to see the bud slowly unwrap itself, and hang down like a little bell.

But she was always very disappointed because the white bells didn't ring.

"They ought to," said Millicent Mary, and she shook each snowdrop to see if she could make it ring. "Bells like this should ring – they really should! Ring, little snowdrop, ring!"

But not one would ring. Still, Millicent Mary wouldn't give it up. Every morning when she put on her hat and coat and went into the garden, she bent down and shook the snowdrops to see if perhaps today they would say ting-a-ling-a-ling. But they never did.

One day she went to her garden when the snow was on the ground. The snowdrops were buried beneath the snow, and Millicent Mary had to scrape the white snow away very gently to find out where her snowdrops were.

At last all the little white bells were showing. She shook them but no sound came. "Well, you might have rung just a tiny tune to tell me you were grateful to me for scraping the snow away!" said Millicent Mary.

She was just going to stand up and go to the shed to fetch her broom when she saw something rather strange. The snow on the bed nearby seemed to be moving itself — poking itself up as if something was underneath it, wriggling hard.

Millicent Mary was surprised. She was even more surprised when she heard a very tiny voice crying, "Help me! Oh, help me!"

"Goodness gracious!" said the little girl. "There's something buried under the snow just there — and it's got a little tiny voice that speaks!"

She began to scrape away the snow, and her soft, gentle fingers found something small and strange under the white blanket. She pulled out — well, guess what she pulled out!

Yes — you guessed right. It was a tiny pixie, a fairy with frozen silver wings and a little shivering body dressed in a cobweb dress.

"Oh, thank you!" said the pixie in a tiny voice, like a bird cheeping. "I was so tired last night that I crept under a dead leaf and fell asleep. And when I awoke this morning I found a great, thick, cold, white blanket all over me – and I couldn't get it off! Just wait till I catch the person who threw this big blanket all over the garden!"

Millicent Mary laughed. "It's snow!" she said. "It isn't a real blanket. You poor little thing, you feel so cold, you are freezing my fingers. I'm going to take you indoors and get you warm."

She tucked the pixie into her pocket and went indoors. She didn't think she would show the fairy to anyone, because she might vanish – and Millicent Mary didn't want her to do that. It was fun having a pixie, not as big as a doll, to warm before the fire!

The pixie sat on the fender and stretched out her frozen toes to the dancing flames. Millicent Mary took a piece of blue silk out of her mother's rag-bag and gave it to the pixie.

"Wrap this round you for a cloak," she said. "It will keep out the frost when you leave me."

The pixie was delighted. She wrapped the bit of blue silk all round her and pulled it close. "I shall get my needle and thread and make this lovely piece of silk into a proper coat with sleeves and buttons and collar," she said. "You are a dear little girl! I love you. Yes, really I do. Is there anything you would like me to give *you*?"

Millicent Mary thought hard. Then she shook her head. "No," she said at last. "There isn't anything at all, really. I've got all the toys I want. I did badly want a dolls' house, but I had one for Christmas. I don't want any sweets because I've got a tin of barley-sugar. I don't want chocolate biscuits because Mummy bought some yesterday. No – I can't think of anything."

The pixie looked most disappointed. "I do wish you'd try to think of something," she said. "Try hard!"

Millicent Mary thought again. Then she smiled. "Well," she said, "there *is* something I'd simply love – but it needs magic to do it, I think. I'd *love* it if my snowdrops could ring on my birthday, which is on February 13th!"

"Oh, that's easily managed!" said the pixie. "I'll work a spell for it. Let me see – what's your name?"

"Millicent Mary," said the little girl.

"Millicent Mary," said the pixie, writing it down in a tiny notebook. "Birthday, 13th February. Wants snowdrops to ring on that day. All right – I'll see to it! And now goodbye, my dear. I'm deliciously warm with this blue silk. See you again some day. Don't forget to listen to your snowdrops on February 13th!"

She skipped up into the air, spread her silvery wings, and flew straight out of the top of the window. Millicent Mary couldn't help feeling tremendously excited. Her birthday would soon be here – and just imagine the snowdrops ringing!

Won't she love to shake each tiny white bell, and hear it ring ting-a-ling-a-ling, ting-a-ling-a-ling! Is *your* name Millicent Mary, by any chance, and is *your* birthday on 13th February? If it is, the snowdrops will ring for you too, without a doubt – so don't forget to shake each little white bell on that day, and hear the tinkling sound they make. What a lovely surprise for all the Millicent Marys!

The engine that ran away

Once there was a lovely wooden engine in the playroom. It was red with a blue funnel and blue wheels, and it had a dear little cab just big enough for a doll to stand inside.

At night the toys always ran to the wooden engine to ask him to give them rides round the playroom. Sometimes a doll would stand inside the cab and drive, sometimes the teddy bear and sometimes the pink rabbit.

But the wooden engine wasn't very friendly. "I don't want to give rides," he grumbled. "Get out of my cab, Teddy. I shall upset you if you try to drive me tonight. I'll run over the edge of the rug and jerk you out."

"Engines are made so that they can run along and pull things and give rides to people," said the teddy bear. "Don't be so bad tempered! It's good for you to run about at night. You'll get fat if you don't!"

"I shan't," said the engine and jerked the teddy bear so hard that he fell out. Then the toys were cross and they *all*

clambered on to the engine and made him carry every one of them.

"I shall run away," said the engine, sulkily. "I *won't* give you rides!" And will you believe it, the very next night he ran out of the playroom, down the passage, out of the garden door and into the garden!

"I'm free, I'm free!" he cried, bumping down the path. "I won't give rides any more. I'll go on a long, long journey by myself and have a lovely time!"

Now, the engine had six wooden wheels, but they were not meant to go over rough stones and tufts of grass. He went over such a big stone that quite suddenly the two back wheels came right off! The engine didn't notice it at first, and then he found that he was going rather clumsily. Oh dear – now he only had four wheels!

He went on down the path and squeezed through a hole in the fence at the bottom of the garden – but that was a silly thing to do because he broke off his funnel! He had to leave it behind, because he couldn't possibly put it on again!

On he went and on. "I feel funny without my funnel," he said to himself. "What shall I do if I ever want to send out smoke? I haven't got a funnel to blow through now!"

He bumped over a field, and suddenly ran into a big rabbit. "Hey there – what do you think *you're* doing?" cried the rabbit, angrily. "You bumped my tail."

"Get out of my way then," said the engine, rudely. That made the rabbit so angry that he chased the engine at top speed. It ran over a brick and oh dear – two more wheels broke off!

"Now I can hardly run at all," said the engine in alarm. "Oh dear, oh dear – four wheels gone, and my funnel, too. What bad luck!"

"To-whit-too-whoo!" said a big owl, flying overhead. "What's this crawling

17

along? A new kind of rat? I'll attack it!"

And down swooped the owl and caught hold of the engine's little cab with its strong feet. The cab broke away in the owl's claws, and the poor engine hurried off without it, scared and trembling. The owl dropped the cab in disgust. "It wasn't a rat after all," it said.

The engine went on and on, and came to a very stony path indeed. Crack! Crack! Both its last wheels broke away, and the engine found itself sliding down a muddy bank, unable to stop itself. Splash! It went into a pond and floated there, looking very strange.

No wheels! No cab! Not even a funnel! Just a flat piece of wood and a round body – nothing else. No wonder the pixie who lived by the bank wondered what was falling down near her home.

"Save me, save me!" called the engine, floating away.

"Good gracious! What can it be?" said the pixie. She got a piece of string and made a loop at one end. She threw the loop over the body part of the engine and drew him back to shore. "Whatever are you?" she said.

"I'm an engine," said the poor, broken toy. "But I've lost my wheels and my cab and my funnel, so I feel very miserable indeed. I've run away, you see."

"Why did you run away?" said the pixie, drying the engine.

"Because I didn't like giving the toys a ride each night," said the engine.

"How mean of you!" said the pixie. "But I suppose you feel happier now that you have lost your six nice wheels and your cab and your lovely funnel. You can't give *anyone* a ride now."

"I *don't* feel happy," said the engine. "It's dreadful to have no wheels. And I hate not having a cab and a funnel. I wish I was back in the playroom, with all the things I've lost. I'd let the toys ride me all night long!"

"Would you really?" said the pixie. "Because if you *really* mean that I'll help you."

"I do mean it," said the engine. "I do, I do!"

Well, the pixie tied the bit of string to the body of the poor old engine and dragged it back the way he had come. First she found two wheels. Then she came to where the owl had dropped the cab. She picked that up, too. Then she found two more wheels, and soon she came to where the little blue funnel lay beside the fence. Up the garden she found the last two wheels.

"There!" she said, "I've found everything you lost. I've some magic with me and I'll put you right if you keep your promise."

"I will, truly I will," said the engine.

And then you should have seen the pixie using her magic! It was rather like blue Vaseline, and she rubbed it on the wheels and the funnel and the cab and stuck them back in their proper places.

Soon the engine felt quite himself again!

"Oh, thank you," he said, gratefully. "I feel like an engine again now. It's lovely. Can I give you a ride?"

"Oh yes!" said the pixie, and she stepped into the little cab. She could drive beautifully! She drove the engine in at the garden door, up the passage and back to the playroom. Well, well – how clever of her!

"Toys! I've brought the runaway engine back to you!" she said. "He's nice and kind now – but if he ever says he won't give you rides, look out! Because then the magic that keeps his wheels and his cab and his funnel on will vanish away – and they will all fall off on to the floor!"

And now the toys take it in turns to drive the wooden engine round and round the playroom every night – and so far he has still got all his wheels and his cab and his funnel. I do hope he doesn't lose them, don't you?

Sammy and the spider

There was once a boy called Sammy who was afraid of spiders. If he saw one running across the room he would squeal in fright.

"Don't be silly, Sammy," said his mother. "A spider can't hurt you!"

"I don't like all its legs," said Sammy.

"But my dear child, a caterpillar has plenty of legs, and you pick those up!" said his mother.

"I know," said Sammy. "But I just don't like spiders. I'm going to stamp on that one and kill it."

"Sammy, don't do that," said his mother. "Why should you take away a spider's life just because you don't happen to like it? I'd be very sorry if somebody was to stamp on *you* just because they didn't like you."

"Well – it does seem unkind," said Sammy. "But let me shoo it out of the room, Mummy!"

His mother got a shovel, let the spider run on to it, and then she dropped it out of the window.

"You must be kind to things even if you don't like them," she said. "Don't turn yourself into somebody cruel and unthinking, when you see something you are afraid of. Don't be afraid of it, and you won't feel unkind!"

"That's difficult," said Sammy. But because he knew that his mother was wise and kind herself, he tried to remember what she said.

Now one day a most enormous spider came into Sammy's bedroom. It really was a *giant*. It had eight legs, of course, and it ran like clockwork on them. Sammy stared at the spider, feeling really afraid.

"I must kill it!" he said to himself.

Then he thought again. "But after all, it can't *help* being a spider. Perhaps it would rather not be. But it has to be because it came out of a spider's egg. I shan't kill it. Mummy's right – it's bad to hurt something just because you don't happen to like it. But what shall I do with it?"

Sammy could not bear to touch the big spider. So he got his cricket bat and let the spider run on to it. Then he took the bat to the window and shook it smartly. The spider dropped off it on to the hedge below. Sammy couldn't see where it went.

"Well, that's good," he thought. "I hope it won't come back again. I'm glad I didn't stamp on it."

No more spiders came into Sammy's room that autumn, and he didn't think any more about them. Then his birthday came, and he was tremendously excited.

He had a new bicycle, with a bell, a basket, and a saddle-bag. That was simply marvellous. He had a football, and he had a toy aeroplane that really flew well.

His uncle sent him a postal order. "Buy yourself a new paintbox," he wrote in a letter. "I know you want one."

"That's just what I *do* want!" said Sammy joyfully. "Mummy, what do I do with this paper money?"

"You take it down to the post office, and they will give you money for it," said Mummy. "Take it tomorrow, because it's Saturday and you will have lots of time."

So Sammy left the paper money in his bedroom till the next day, and a dreadful thing happened! The wind came in at the window, took hold of the paper money and whisked it right away!

Sammy ran to catch it – but the wind took it out of the window at the top, where it was open. Sammy gave a yell. There was his paper money flying away on the wind!

He tore downstairs to find it. He rushed into the garden and looked on the ground everywhere. But the paper money had quite disappeared. It was a great shock for poor Sammy.

"Darling, it's no good looking any more," said Mummy, at last. "It will have blown miles away by now. There is such a tremendous wind today. Never mind. You have lots of lovely presents, and maybe someone will give you a paintbox for Christmas."

All the same Sammy was very, very sad. It was dreadful to lose the money. He had felt so rich – and now he felt so poor.

He went out into the garden to play with his football. He kicked it high into the air, and it landed on top of the privet hedge. Sammy went to get it.

And he saw a most strange and amazing sight. There was a very large web on the hedge, made by a giant of a spider, who was lurking at one end. No flies had been caught in the web – but

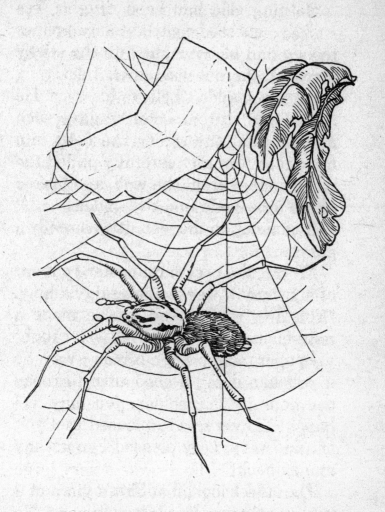

something else had been caught! Yes – you've guessed right! Sammy's paper money had blown right into the sticky web, and there it was, safely held.

Sammy couldn't believe his eyes. He stared and stared. Then he gave such a shout that the spider ran deep into the hedge. Sammy carefully pulled the paper money from the web, and looked to see if he could find the spider.

It came up to the web. It was really a *giant*.

"You're the very same spider I put out of my window weeks ago!" said Sammy. "You are, really. And you've made a marvellous web – and that web caught my paper money when it blew away. So if you like doing a good turn to repay one done to you, spider, you may feel happy! I'm very, very pleased I let you go, and very, very pleased I've got my money back!"

The spider looked at Sammy. Then it ran into the middle of its web.

"I'm not afraid of you any more," said

Sammy. "Not one single bit. You're a friend, not an enemy! You've saved my money. I shall always like spiders after this!"

He ran indoors to tell his mother. She was simply delighted. "Well, one good turn deserves another," she said, "but I'm sure it isn't often that a spider can do a thing like *that*, Sammy!"

Sammy got his paintbox, and now he is going in for every painting competition. I wonder if he will win a prize, don't you?

The robber who wasn't there

It was a lovely spring day, and the sun shone down warmly. The primroses began to open in the garden, and George and Nora went to pick a bunch for the playroom table.

Happy, their dog, went with them. He ran round the garden, smelling here and there, just as happy as his name. He ran to the garden shed and sniffed around.

Suddenly he cocked up his ears and then began to bark madly! How he barked!

"Woof, woof, woof! Woof, woof, woof!"

"Whatever's the matter, Happy?" cried Nora, in surprise. "You'll bark your head off, then what will you do?"

"Woof, woof, woof!" barked Happy, and he scraped at the shed door with his paw.

"He wants to go in," said George. "I wonder why?"

Happy stopped barking and stood listening to something inside the shed, his head well on one side. The children listened too.

There was a noise inside the shed! It was a funny noise — a kind of scrapy, scrambly noise — and then a pot fell over and broke!

The children jumped and looked scared.

"Woof, woof, woof!" barked Happy again, and he scraped at the wooden door as if he would like to break it down.

"There's somebody hiding in there," said Nora.

"Who could it be?" said George, in a frightened whisper.

"A robber!" whispered back Nora. "Oh dear, George, I feel frightened. Let's go and tell Mummy."

They waited for a moment, and then they heard the noise inside the shed again. Another pot fell over, and the children jumped and ran away. Happy stayed behind, barking, and pawing at the door.

"There's one thing – the robber won't escape from the shed whilst Happy is barking outside," panted George, as the two children ran to the house.

"No – so he's a prisoner till we get somebody to catch him!" said Nora.

They rushed into the house and called for their mother. "Mummy! Mummy! Come quickly! Where are you?"

But Mummy was out. So they ran to tell Jane their big sister. "Jane! Jane! There's a robber in the garden shed!" said George. "Will you come and catch him?"

"Good gracious, no!" cried Jane, quite alarmed. "I'm certainly not going robber-catching! I'll tell Cook!"

So Jane, George and Nora ran to the kitchen to tell the cook about the robber in the garden shed. Cook was surprised to see them all running at top speed into her kitchen.

"What's the matter?" she said.

"Oh, Cook, there's a robber in the garden shed!" panted Jane. "Get your rolling pin and come and catch him."

"Indeed, I won't," said Cook at once. "A robber should be caught by the policeman. He'll be by here soon. We'll watch for him and tell him. Fancy that now – a robber in the garden shed!"

"Happy is keeping him prisoner till we get somebody to catch the robber," said Nora, feeling tremendously excited. "Can't you hear him barking like mad?"

They could. "Woof, woof, woof!"

"Here comes the policeman!" said Cook at last, and they saw the big burly policeman walking slowly down their road. George, Nora, Jane, and Cook all flew out to the front gate and called to him.

"Oh, Mr Policeman! We've got a robber here!"

"What did you say?" asked the policeman in great surprise, and he took out his notebook and pencil.

"Oh, there's no time to be writing notes," cried Jane. "There's a robber in the garden shed and the dog's guarding him. He'll be a very fierce robber, and maybe he'll fight you, Mr Policeman. Hadn't you better get someone to help you?"

"Oh no," said the policeman, rather grandly. "I'm quite used to robbers."

So George, Nora, Jane, Cook, and the policeman all went down the garden to the shed, where Happy was still barking.

"Now just listen, everyone!" said George.

So they all listened, and sure enough they could hear the noise in the shed all right – and two more pots fell over with a crash! Even the policeman jumped, and as for Jane, she ran half-way up the garden in fright.

"Now here's a strange thing," said

the policeman, suddenly pointing to the door. "It's locked on the outside, there's the key in the lock, and it's turned! Now how did the robber get in there, and yet lock the door on the outside?"

Everybody stared at the lock, but nobody could think how a robber could lock himself in and yet leave the key outside. It was a mystery.

The policeman unlocked the door and shouted out in a loud, stern voice, "Come out, there! Come out at once!"

Everyone waited to see who would come out – but nobody did! Another plant pot fell over. The policeman grew angry.

"Am I to come in after you? Come out at once!" But still nobody came out. So the policeman bravely stuck his head inside the dark shed and looked around.

"There's nobody here!" he said in the greatest astonishment. "Well – that's odd!"

Everybody looked inside – and sure

enough there was no robber there at all. Happy darted round and round the shed, sniffing happily. Everyone went out again and talked hard.

"Then who made that noise?"

"There *was* somebody there!"

"And it must have been a robber!"

"How could he have got away?"

And suddenly they heard the noise again! They all stared at the door, feeling quite scared.

Then the robber walked out! Yes — he really did! And who do you suppose it was? Why, nobody else but Crawler, the old tortoise, who had been put there asleep in a box for the winter! He had woken up, scrambled out of his box, and crawled round the shed, knocking over pots as he went. Well, well, well!

He walked out into the warm spring sunshine, and blinked his eyes at everyone. Happy danced round him, barking. Everyone went red and looked foolish.

Then George laughed — and Nora

joined in. Jane giggled and Cook roared. The policeman opened his mouth and ha-ha-ha'd too. It was surprising to hear them, and Crawler the tortoise was frightened. He popped his head under his shell!

"The robber who wasn't there!" cried Nora, pointing to the tortoise. "Oh, Crawler, what a fright you gave us!"

A pair of pickles

Billy and Bessie were a pair of pickles. You never knew what mischief they would be up to next!

They dirtied their clothes every day. They lost things. They came in muddy and never thought of wiping their shoes. Well, really, I can't tell you half the things they did, because I would need about ten books to put them in!

Everybody called them "the Pickles". "Where are those Pickles?" Mummy would say at dinner time. "It is time they were home."

"Hello, Pickles!" people would say. Billy and Bessie thought it was fun to be two pickles. They didn't think of the worry they made for their mother.

Now one day a funny little fellow came wandering into our land. He was helper to Mister Grumpy-Wumps, the enchanter of Heyho Wood, and Mister Grumpy-Wumps was in one of his tempers.

He always was on Mondays, because he had cold meat for dinner, and he hated it.

"Cold meat again!" he would shout to his helper. "How dare you!"

"Well, it's Monday," said the helper. "And everyone has cold meat on Monday, sir."

"Well, give me something nice to eat with it!" shouted the enchanter. So sometimes the helper gave him beetroot, sometimes he gave him tomato sauce or celery, and sometimes horseradish and cream.

And then one day Mister Grumpy-Wumps took it into his head to want pickles!

"Pickles!" said the helper in surprise. "I've never heard of them. Can't have pickles, Mister Grumpy-Wumps!"

"How dare you tell me that I can't have something I want!" roared Grumpy-Wumps, and for a moment he looked so fierce that he quite startled the little helper. "Go out and bring me pickles. Don't dare to come back till you've got them!"

"Where do I get them?" asked the helper, putting on his hat.

"How do I know?" said the enchanter. "They may grow on trees. They may be sold in a shop. They may sit on chimney-pots. They may walk about in the fields. Anyway, go and get some."

So that was how the little helper happened to come wandering into our land, looking for pickles. And it so happened that he met Bessie and Billy, who were in mischief as usual, paddling in the muddy pond.

"Hello!" said the little fellow.

"Hello!" said the Pickles.

"I'm looking for something," said the

helper. "Can you help me, I wonder? I'm looking for pickles."

Billy laughed. "*We* are pickles!" he said.

"Don't be silly," said the little man sharply.

"I'm not silly," said Billy. "Anybody will tell you we're pickles. Go and ask that lady over there."

The lady was the wife of the farmer. The little man went over to her and raised his hat politely. "Could you please tell me if those two children are pickles?" he asked.

"They certainly are!" said the farmer's wife, with a smile. "Real pickles!"

"Thank you," said the helper, puzzled. So the children *were* pickles. Well, well, well! He would have to take them to Mister Grumpy-Wumps, that's all.

So he went back to them and took them firmly by the hands. "You must come with me," he said. "My master, Mister Grumpy-Wumps, always has cold meat for his dinner on Mondays, and today is Monday, and he told me to go and get him pickles to eat with his dinner. So I'm afraid you must come."

"We won't! We won't!" cried Bessie. "We're not the kind of pickles you eat! Let us go!"

But the helper wouldn't. No, he made the two Pickles go with him to his own land, and he took them right to the enchanter's castle and led them up to Mister Grumpy-Wumps.

"I've brought you the Pickles," he said.

The enchanter stared at the children in dismay. He was really a very kind-hearted fellow, and he knew he couldn't possibly eat this sort of pickle. Well, well! To think that children were pickles! What a very astonishing thing!

"Please don't think we're pickles to eat," said Billy. "We're not!"

"That lady you pointed out to me said you *were*!" said the helper. "She said you were real pickles."

"Well," said the enchanter, going

rather red, "somehow I don't feel like pickles today. Take the children back, you silly man and when I feel like pickles again, you can fetch them. But today I really don't. I think I'll have beetroot instead."

"How you do change your mind!" grumbled the helper, going to fetch the beetroot. As soon as he was out of the room the children ran through another door and tore home as fast as ever they could. They didn't know how glad Mister Grumpy-Wumps was to see them go! Good gracious! How could anyone eat pickles like that!

When they got home the children sat down quietly in a corner. "I'm going to stop being naughty enough to be called a pickle," whispered Bessie to Billy. "After all, we do upset Mummy when we get so dirty and our clothes so torn. Let's be good for a change."

So now they are really very good, and Mummy can't imagine why. She also doesn't know where one of her jars of home-made pickles has gone to, that the children begged from her. But *I* know! It's hidden inside a hollow tree ready to give to the little helper if ever he comes hunting for pickles again.

"He shan't make a mistake *next* time!" says Billy. What a treat for old Grumpy-Wumps when he tastes *real* pickles!

Mollie's mud-pies

It was very hot, so hot that Mollie wore only a swimsuit. It was nearly summer, and Mummy said if it was so hot now, whatever would it be like in the middle of summer.

"It's nice," said Mollie, who liked wearing almost nothing. She didn't even wear shoes in the garden. "I like it, Mummy. I do wish we were by the sea, then I could swim."

"Well, I'll tell you what I will do," said her mother. "I will water you each night before you go to bed!"

"Water me!" said Mollie, in surprise. "What do you mean, Mummy?"

"Just what I say," said Mummy. "I'll fill a can with half-warm water, and then water you before you go to bed. That will be fun for you."

"Oh, *yes*," said Mollie in delight. "I should love that."

She played in the hot garden. The grass looked yellow, not green. Everywhere was dried up and dusty. Mollie wondered if the birds had any puddles to drink from. They must be thirsty now, with all the puddles dried up. So she filled a little bowl with water, and set it out on the grass. It was fun to see the birds coming to drink from it.

"They drink so sweetly," said Mollie. "They dip in their beaks, and then hold their heads back, Mummy, and let the water run down their throats."

When the evening came, Mummy filled a big watering-can with half-warm water, and called Mollie. "Come and have your watering!"

"Will it make me grow, like the flowers?" cried Mollie, dancing about. Mummy tipped up the can. Mollie gave a squeal. Although the water was not cold, it felt cold on her hot little body. She danced about, squeaking with excitement and joy.

"The water's made a nice muddy patch on the path," she cried. "Look, my toes are brown and muddy with dancing in it."

"You'll have to wash them well," said Mummy, filling the can again. "Come along – one more watering and you must go to bed."

The patch of path was indeed wet and muddy after the second can of water had been poured all over Mollie. "If it's wet tomorrow, I shall make little mud-pies of it," said Mollie.

It was still muddy the next day. After breakfast Mollie went to the mud and dabbled her fingers in it. "I shall make little pies and cakes of mud, and set them in the sun to dry," she thought. "That will be a nice game to play."

Mummy called her. "If you want to play that dirty game you must wear an overall over that nice clean swimsuit. Come along."

Mollie ran indoors. When she came out again she found someone else in her mud-patch! It was a little bird with a touch of white at the foot of his dark, long tail, and underneath his body. He stared at Mollie, and then scraped up some mud in his beak.

"Oh!" said Mollie, pleased. "Are you making mud-pies too? I never knew a bird liked playing with mud before. Do play with me."

The little bird gave a twitter, filled his beak quite full, and then suddenly darted into the air on curving wings.

Mollie saw that he had a forked tail behind him.

"I wish he hadn't gone," she thought. "It would have been fun to play with him. I suppose he has taken the mud to make mud-pies somewhere else."

Suddenly the little bird came back again. He looked at Mollie, and she looked at him. He wondered if Mollie was the kind of child to throw stones at him, or to shout and frighten him away.

But she wasn't. She was like you. She liked birds, and wanted them to stay close to her so that she could watch them and make friends with them.

She sat quite still and watched him. He went to the mud again, and began to scrape up some more. Then another bird, exactly like him, flew down, and he began to dabble in it as well. Mollie was delighted.

"Everyone is making mud-pies this morning," she said. "Gracious – here's another! How busy they all are in my muddy patch. I'll get busy too."

Once the birds had made up their minds that Mollie was a friend, they became very busy indeed. They filled their little beaks with mud time after time, and then flew away round the house. Mollie wondered where they went. They kept coming and going all the morning.

"Funny little mud-pie birds," she said to them. "Do you bake your mud-pies up on the roof somewhere? I bake mine here, look!"

The hot sun baked her pies beautifully. She put them on a plate out of her tea-set and took them in to her mummy.

"Have a mud-pie?" she said. "They are lovely. And, oh, Mummy, the mud-pie birds have played in the mud with me all morning. They were sweet."

Mummy was surprised. "Mud-pie birds! Whatever do you mean?"

"Well, they came and played with my mud and took some away to make mud-pies with. I expect they baked them up on the roof," said Mollie.

Mummy thought it was a little tale of Mollie's. She pretended to eat Mollie's mud-pie, and then offered Mollie a bun from the oven.

"I've been baking too," she said. "Have a hot bun? And now I think you had better stop playing with the mud and wash yourself."

"The mud is gone now," said Mollie. "The sun has baked it hard."

The little birds didn't come into the garden any more that day. "I suppose they only came for the mud," thought Mollie. "Well, if Mummy waters me again tonight there will be more mud tomorrow for us all to play with."

There was – a nice big patch – and down came the little birds again, to scrape up the mud. Mollie was so pleased.

"It's nice to have you to play with me," she said to the busy little birds. "But I really wish you would tell me what you do with your mud."

They twittered a little song to her, high and sweet, but she didn't understand what they said. They flew to and from the mud all morning, till the sun dried it up.

"Mummy, why do the mud-pie birds take my mud?" asked Mollie. "I do want to know. I didn't know that birds like mud so much."

Her daddy was there, and he looked up from his newspaper. "What's all this about mud-pie birds?" he asked. So Mollie told him.

"Ah," he said. "Now I know what birds you mean. Your mud-pie birds are house-martins, cousins of the pretty swallows we see flying high in the air all summer."

"House-martins!" said Mollie. "*I* should call them mud-martins. What do they do with my mud?"

"Come with me and I'll show you," said Daddy. He took Mollie's hand, and led her upstairs. They went into her

bedroom. Daddy went to the window and opened it wide.

"Now look out of your window, above it, to the edge of the roof overhead," he said. "Tell me what you see."

Mollie leaned out, and looked up. She gave a cry. "Oh, Daddy! The mud-pie birds are there. They are making something of my mud. What is it?"

"It's a nest," said Daddy. "The house-martins don't use dead leaves and twigs and moss for their nests as most birds do. They make them of mud. They fetch beakfuls of mud, and plaster it against the wall, gradually building it out till they have made a fine nest of mud, with a hole to get in and out. There's the hole in that nest. Look!"

As Mollie watched, one of the little birds flew up with his beak full of mud from somewhere, and pressed it against the edge of his nest.

"There you are," said Daddy. "He brings wet mud, and it dries hard in the sun, making a perfectly good nest for his little wife to lay her eggs in, and have her young ones."

"Oh, Daddy! Fancy making a nest of my mud, the mud that was made when Mummy watered me each evening," said Mollie in delight. "I couldn't think why the mud-birds came to make mud-pies. I did not know they were making mud-nests – and over my bedroom window, too, tucked under the edge of the roof! I shall hear them calling and twittering to each other all day long. Look – there's another nest farther along. You won't pull them down, will you?"

56

"Of course not!" said Daddy, who was fond of birds. "They can nest there in peace and happiness, out of reach of the cats. Later on we shall see their young ones popping their heads out of the holes in the mud-nests."

And so they did! The house-martins laid eggs in their strange mud-nests, and in a few weeks' time Mollie saw three or four tiny feathery heads popping out of the hole in the nest above her window, waiting for the father and mother to come back with flies to feed them.

Later still the little birds flew into the sky with their mother and father, learning how to dart and soar and glide, and how to catch the hundreds of insects that flew in the air. Daddy said they did a great deal of good, because the flies were a pest.

And then one day they were all gone. Mollie looked into the sky and they were not there.

"They've gone away south, where it

is warmer," said Daddy. "There will be plenty of insects for them to eat there. Our winter is coming and they do not like that."

"I don't want them to go away," said Mollie sadly.

"Well, they will be back again in the spring," said Daddy. "And, Mollie, if the weather is hot and dry again when they come back, you must make a muddy patch once more, and they will come to it, and build their nest again over your window. They love to come back to exactly the same place, if they can."

So, of course, Mollie is going to watch for them when the spring comes. You must watch too, and if we have hot and dry weather in May, when the mud-pie birds want to build their nests, you can do as Mollie did – make a muddy patch for them, and watch them fly down to it to fill their beaks.

Maybe they will build a mud-nest over your window, too. That really would be fun, wouldn't it?

Tiptap's little trick

Mr Twisty went to market every Friday with two big baskets of goods to sell. In one basket he took vegetables or fruit, and in the other he took eggs.

"Old Twisty helps himself to other people's fruit and vegetables and eggs at night," said the people of the village. "He comes in the dark, like a shadow – and pulls up our lettuces and picks our peas and our fruit. He goes into our hen-houses and takes the eggs, as sly as a rat in the night!"

But nobody could catch old Twisty at it, nobody at all. He was as full of tricks and wily ways as a weasel.

"We'll have to play a trick on *him*,"

said Dame Ho-Ho at last. "So let's think hard."

They thought and they thought. Mr Flap frowned and Mr Flop scowled, they thought so hard. Mother Run-Round and old Mrs Scatter did their best to think of a way to trick Twisty and pay him back for his mean ways.

It was little Tiptap who thought of an idea. He told the others, and they laughed. "It's a bit silly," said Dame Ho-Ho, "but it *might* catch him."

"It's good," said Mr Flap. "We'll try it."

So the next day, when everyone was going to market, little Tiptap went, too. He had some strong rope coiled round his waist, and he laughed as he went.

He ran round a corner, tied the end of the rope to something there, and then came back again, holding his end. He waited till he saw Mr Twisty coming along with two heavy baskets.

Then Tiptap began to tug and pull at the rope for all he was worth. "Come up, there!" he yelled. "Come along, will you! Why won't you come? You'll be late for market and I won't be able to sell you. Come on, there!"

Mr Twisty stopped, put down his baskets and watched. He liked seeing people in difficulties.

Tiptap tugged and tugged at the rope which was stretched as tight as could be. "Come along, I tell you!" he cried. "Acting like this on market day!"

"Ha-ha!" laughed Mr Twisty. "Ho-ho! Your pig – or your cow or whatever it is – wants to go a different way from you. Ho-ho! He'll pull *you* round the corner soon!"

Everyone was watching Tiptap. Dame Ho-Ho was there, smiling. Mr Flap and Mr Flop stood there, nodding in delight. Mother Run-Round and Mrs Scatter laughed loudly.

"All of you laughing at me and not giving a hand to help!" cried Tiptap, pulling hard. "Help, somebody!"

Mother Run-Round came up to help.

She tugged and pulled, too, but it wasn't any good. No animal came round the corner on the end of the rope.

"*Will* you come along?" shouted Tiptap, in a very angry voice. "I tell you, if you don't come I'll sell you for five pounds, here and now! I'm tired of you!"

Twisty pricked up his ears. What! Tiptap was so angry that he would sell this animal cheaply? Well, perhaps Twisty could get a good bargain.

"Here – I'll pull it round for you," he said. "And, if you like, I'll buy the creature. It will save you going to the market. But a stubborn, bad-tempered animal like this won't be worth much."

"You're right," said Tiptap, tugging. "If it's going to act like this at every corner I'll never get to market. You can have it for five pounds."

"Say three," said Twisty, and he took the rope-end from Tiptap. He pulled. My word – what animal could there be at the end of this rope? He couldn't budge

it! It must at least be a cow – or even a horse or donkey! He tugged and tugged. Yes – it must be a horse.

"Say four pounds," said Tiptap, "and your two baskets of goods. You won't want to carry those to market if you've got something else to tug along."

"A horse for four pounds!" thought Twisty in delight, still pulling hard. He turned to Tiptap.

"All right. Feel in my pocket and take four pounds. You can have the baskets, too."

"Thanks!" said Tiptap, and winked at everyone in delight. He picked up the baskets and looked into them. "Ah – these eggs must be yours, Mr Flap and Mr Flop. And these lettuces must belong to you, Mother Run-Round. They are just like you grow. And these . . ."

"You stop talking like that!" yelled Mr Twisty, in a rage. But he couldn't run after Tiptap because he didn't dare to leave go of the rope!

Tiptap and the others went off giggling. Mr Twisty nearly went mad trying to pull the rope hard enough to pull the animal to him.

Suddenly someone appeared at the corner. It was Mr Letters, the postman. He shouted at Mr Twisty.

"Hey, you! What do you think you're doing? You've nearly pulled the letter-box down. Is this a joke, or what?"

Mr Twisty stared at him. He ran quickly to the corner and looked round it. My, oh my – that rope was tied firmly round a stout red letter-box – and it was almost bent in half with Twisty's pulling! He gaped at it.

"B-b-b-but there should be a horse, or a cow or a pig, on the end of the rope," stammered Mr Twisty in dismay.

"Well, it must have turned into a letter-box, then," said Mr Letters. "And I'm afraid I must ask you to come to the police-station with me, Mr Twisty, on a charge of doing malicious damage to a public letter-box! That's for posting letters in, not for pulling down!"

Mr Twisty didn't wait a moment. He fled at top speed, caught the first bus he saw, and went to the Village of Far-Away. What with animals that turned into letter-boxes – and postmen that wanted to take him away – and everyone laughing at him – he just couldn't stay another moment.

The folk of the village saw him going by at top speed to catch the bus. How they laughed!

Tiptap divided the four pounds between everyone who had goods stolen from them by Twisty. And what do you think they did with it? They put it together again and gave a party for Tiptap!

"You got rid of mean old Twisty," they said. "You deserve a party, Tiptap. He'll never dare to come back again."

They were right. He never did.

Lazy little Pimmy

Pimmy was the pixie who lived in Pimmy Cottage at the end of Snapdragon Village. You could tell he was lazy because his garden was full of weeds, his windows were dirty, and his gate hung crooked.

Now one day it was very, very windy. Pimmy put on his red hat with the feather in it and went out. It was a silly hat to wear on a windy day, but Pimmy liked it very much. It was his best hat, and the feather made him feel grand.

The wind saw Pimmy's hat in delight. *Whooooo!* Just the kind of hat the wind liked to play with. It swept down on Pimmy, swished off his hat, and made it sail high in the air.

"Oh – bother, bother, bother!" cried Pimmy, as he saw his lovely hat whirled away. "Come back hat!"

But the hat didn't. It was enjoying itself. It sailed off, went over a tree, and then came down on the top of the shed in Dame Stern's garden.

"That's a nuisance," said Pimmy, screwing up his nose. "I daren't go and get my hat off Dame Stern's shed without asking her – and she may snap my head off, she's so bad-tempered."

Anyway, he went to ask if he might get it, because he really couldn't bear to lose such a lovely hat. He knocked on Dame Stern's door.

"If it's the washing, leave it on the step!" called a voice.

"It isn't," said Pimmy.

"Well, if it's the paper boy, bring me the right paper tomorrow, or I'll chase you all the way down the street and back again," said the voice.

Pimmy felt glad he wasn't the paper boy.

"It isn't the paper boy," he said. "It's Pimmy. My hat has been blown on top of your shed, Dame Stern, and please may I get it?"

"No, you may not," said Dame Stern. "You'll fall off and break your neck."

"I could climb up a ladder all right," said Pimmy politely.

"I haven't got a ladder," said Dame Stern. "But Old Man Stamper has. You might be able to borrow his."

Pimmy went off to Old Man Stamper's house. The old fellow was in his garden, digging.

"Please, Mister Stamper, could you lend me your ladder?" said Pimmy. "My hat's blown on to the top of Dame Stern's shed."

"What a silly hat to have," said Old Man Stamper. "Well – I'll lend you my ladder, but you must do something for me first. You run along to Mother Grumble's and ask her to let me have a little of her cough medicine. My cough's so bad at night."

Pimmy didn't want to go to Mother Grumble's. It was a long way to go, and he was afraid of her. But still, he wouldn't get the ladder if he didn't, and if he didn't get the ladder, he'd lose his hat. So he had to go.

He came to Mother Grumble's and knocked at the door. He could hear the old lady grumbling away to someone.

"And if it isn't one thing, it's another. One of my hens got loose this morning, and it pecked up all my lettuce, and then a stray dog came and dug up my carrot bed, and . . ."

Pimmy knocked again.

"And now here's someone come to the door, just as I've got settled down to have a cup of tea! Really, if it isn't one thing, it's another. Who's at the door? Speak up!"

"Pimmy the Pixie!" called Pimmy. "Please will you lend Old Man Stamper some of your cough medicine?"

"Well, if he isn't asking all day long for something or other!" said Mother

Grumble. "First it's a pinch of tea, then it's a box of matches, and now it's cough medicine. I haven't got a bottle to put some in for him. You'd better go and ask the chemist to let you have one, Pimmy. Then I'll give you some."

Pimmy groaned. The chemist lived over the other side of the hill. He set off again and came to the chemist.

"Hello, lazy little Pimmy," said the chemist, who had once had Pimmy for an errand boy and sent him away because he was so lazy. "What do *you* want?"

"Could you let me have an old medicine bottle for Mother Grumble?" said Pimmy.

"Ah, you want something for nothing, do you?" said the chemist. "No, no – if you want a bottle, you must do something to get it, Pimmy. I don't give something for nothing!"

"Well, what shall I do?" said Pimmy, feeling that he would never get home that day.

"See this parcel?" said the chemist. "Well, you take it to Mrs Flap's for me, and when you come back you shall have the bottle. See?"

Pimmy set off. Mrs Flap's house was half a mile away. Pimmy wished he had had his shoes mended the week before, as he should have done. There was a hole in one, and the stones kept coming in and hurting his foot.

He came to Mrs Flap's. Nobody answered the door. Pimmy knocked and knocked, more and more loudly. Then the window of the next house flew up, and an angry face looked out.

"What's all this noise? It sounds like a thousand postmen at the door – *knock*, *knock*, *knock*! Mrs Flap's not in. She's out shopping."

"Oh, dear," said Pimmy, looking at the angry face of Mr Glum. "I've come so far to bring her a parcel from the chemist."

"Well, I'll take it in for you if you'll do

something for me," said Mr Glum. "My dog hasn't been for his walk today, and he's longing for it. My leg's bad, and I can't take him. You just take him round the streets and back again, and when you come back I'll take the parcel in for Mrs Flap. Then you won't need to sit on her doorstep and wait."

"I don't like taking dogs for walks," said Pimmy. "And besides, I'm tired."

Mr Glum looked at him hard. "Ah, you're lazy little Pimmy, aren't you?" he said. "*You* wouldn't take a dog for a walk, no matter how hard he begged you, would you? You're too lazy."

He slammed down his window. Pimmy stared at it in despair. Mrs Flap might be hours before she came back from her shopping. He couldn't wait all that time. He would have to take Mr Glum's dog for a walk, even though his legs felt dreadfully tired.

So he shouted out loudly: "Mr Glum, Mr Glum, I'll take your dog out!"

The front door opened. Mr Glum

limped out with a very large dog on a lead. "Here you are," he said. "Take him for a nice run and come back again."

Pimmy took the lead and set off. He meant to go round the corner and sit down for ten minutes, and then take the dog home again. But the dog had other ideas.

Pimmy didn't take that dog for a run – it took Pimmy for a gallop. It was a large dog and a strong dog, and a very determined dog. It tore off down the street, and Pimmy was dragged after it.

"Here! Hi! Whoa!" panted Pimmy. But the dog took not the slightest notice. It rushed on like an express train, and Pimmy had to follow it. He ran and he ran, and he panted and he puffed. He had never in his life run so fast.

Then the dog suddenly turned and ran back to sniff an exciting smell. The lead wound itself round Pimmy's legs, and he sat down very suddenly. The dog

looked surprised and sniffed at Pimmy's ear.

"Don't, you horrid dog," panted Pimmy. "What do you mean by rushing off at top speed like that? Don't sniff in my ear – it tickles."

The dog sniffed at Pimmy's nose. Pimmy got up, and the dog at once started off at top speed again. But, luckily, this time it made for home. Pimmy tore along behind it, almost falling over his own feet.

He got back to Mr Glum's, his face hot and red, his breath coming in such loud pants that Mr Glum heard him before he even saw him. Mr Glum smiled one of his rare smiles.

"I see Scamper has been giving you a good run," he said. "Well, it will do you good, lazy little Pimmy. Here, here, Scamper! Come in. Where is the parcel you wanted me to give to Mrs Flap? Ah, there she is. You can give it to her yourself now."

He shut his door; Pimmy glared at it.

So he had taken that dreadful dog out for nothing! He scowled, gave the parcel to Mrs Flap, and set off wearily to the chemist's.

"What a long time you've been!" said the chemist. "Lazy as usual, I suppose – just crawled along, didn't you?"

"I've been rushing along at about sixty miles an hour!" said Pimmy, crossly, and he took the bottle the chemist held out to him. "Thank you. If I'd known how many miles I'd have had to run when I took that parcel for you, I wouldn't have done it!"

Pimmy took the bottle to Mother Grumble. She got up to fill it, grumbling away as usual. "If it isn't one thing, it's another. No sooner do I sit myself down than up I have to get again for lazy little fellows like you, Pimmy!"

Pimmy took the bottle of cough medicine to Old Man Stamper. The old man was very glad to have it. He took a dose at once.

"Could I borrow your ladder, please?"

said Pimmy. "You said I could if I brought you some cough medicine."

"Dear me, I'd forgotten," said Old Man Stamper. "There it is, look. Mind you bring it back."

Pimmy took the ladder. It was heavy. He staggered back to Dame Stern's garden.

"Oh, you've got the ladder, have you?" said Dame Stern. "Now you be careful not to tread on any of my beds, Pimmy!"

Pimmy was very careful. His arms ached with the heavy ladder and he was glad to put it up against the shed. He went up. Now at last, at last, he would get his lovely hat!

But it wasn't there! It was gone! Pimmy burst into tears. Dame Stern was surprised.

"What's the matter?" she called. "Oh, of course, your hat is gone. Yes, I saw it go. The wind came down and swept it away. I don't know where it went to."

Pimmy cried bitterly. He carried the heavy ladder back to Old Man Stamper.

Then he went home, still crying. And when he got there, what did he see in his very own garden but his lovely hat, feather and all!

"Oh – who brought you back?" he cried in delight, and put it on. The wind swept round him and shouted in his ear.

"I brought it back here, Pimmy. I was just playing a trick on you, that's all. I brought it back!"

"Oh, you mean, unkind wind!" cried Pimmy. "I've borrowed a heavy ladder and carried it ever so far – I've fetched cough medicine – I've carried a parcel – and I've taken a dog out for a run – all to get my hat, and now it's here! I'm tired out!"

"Do you good, do you good, lazy little Pimmy!" said the wind, and tried to pull his hat off again. "Do you good! *Whoooo-ooo-ooo!*"

Little black bibs

There was once a flock of young sparrows who were very hungry in the winter. Snow was on the ground, the puddles were frozen, and the trees had no berries left on them. So there was nothing to eat or drink.

Old Dame Kind-Heart saw them looking very thin and miserable one day. So she made a fine pudding of millet seeds, crusts of bread and old biscuits. "This will feed those young sparrows well!" she said to herself. "I'll make a pudding like this each day, and feed them all."

So the next day she rang a little bell and all the sparrows lined up ready for their meal.

"Girls first, and boys after," said Dame Kind-Heart, who was very strict about manners.

So the girl-sparrows lined up and hopped in at the window one by one, pecking up the spoonful of pudding that Dame Kind-Heart offered them.

Then the boys came, and they gobbled up their share too. The line of sparrows seemed never-ending. The pudding didn't last till the end of the line!

"Dear me! Who would have thought there were so many young sparrows?" said Dame Kind-Heart. "I must make a bigger pudding tomorrow."

She didn't know that after they had all had their turn, the girl-sparrows lined up behind the boys, and then when they had had *their* turn, the boys lined up behind the girls again!

You see, both boy and girl-sparrows were exactly alike, so poor Dame Kind-Heart couldn't possibly know which were which. She just thought there must be an extraordinary number of boy-sparrows, coming along in a never-ending line after the girl-sparrows had been fed!

But her next door neighbour, Mister Sharp, told her of the trick that was being played on her, and she was cross.

"Naughty little things," she said. "Well, I will make sure it doesn't happen again!" And that night she got out a pot of black paint, cleaned a little brush and set them ready for the morning.

In the morning, when the sparrows lined up again, she called to them. "Fly into my room for a minute please, boy-sparrows."

When they were all inside, Dame Kind-Heart dabbed a bib of black paint under the chins of all the surprised boy-sparrows. "There!" she said, "now I shall know the girls from the boys! The girls have no bibs – but you boys have little black ones. You can't trick me any more!"

They couldn't, of course, so each sparrow had his or her share of the pudding, and no more. It was quite enough for them too.

The funny thing is that the cock-sparrows still wear their little black bibs, and the hens have none. Do look and see, when next you go out in the garden.

Goodbye Master Meddle

Meddle always liked roaming round the railway station. It was a most exciting place, with trains puffing in and out, people hurrying all about, and porters shouting, "Mind your backs, please!"

One morning he went into the station, and sat down on a seat to watch what was going on. He saw the people buying their tickets, carrying their luggage, looking for their trains.

"They all look very *worried*," said Meddle to himself. "Very worried indeed. Perhaps I'd better help some of them."

Now, Meddle, as you know, was exactly like his name. If he *could* poke his long nose into anything and meddle with it, he was happy! So up he got to see what he could do.

He met a little man panting and puffing, carrying a very heavy bag. Meddle went up to him and tried to get hold of it. "Let me help," he said.

"Certainly not. Let go," said the man, fiercely. "I know what you'd do if I let you take my bag – run off with it! And that's the last I would see of it."

"What a dreadful thing to say!" said Meddle, and stalked off crossly. He bumped into a woman who was carrying three parcels and dragging a little dog along too. "Allow me, Madam!" said Meddle politely, and took the biggest parcel from the woman.

The dog immediately flew at him and nipped his leg. Meddle dropped the parcel and howled. There was a crash!

"There now!" said the woman, angrily. "I had my best glass bowls packed in that parcel! What do you

think you are doing, snatching it from me?"

"Your horrible dog bit me," said Meddle, most annoyed.

"Well, of course he did!" said the woman. "He thought you were stealing my parcel. It served you right. Please call a porter and ask him to clear up this mess of broken glass – and you will have to pay me five pounds for breaking the bowls."

A porter came up. "*I* saw you meddling!" he said to Meddle. "If parcels want carrying, *I'll* carry them. It's my job, not yours. And *you* can clear up the mess, because that's your job, not mine!"

Well, you would have thought that Meddle would have had enough of poking his nose into other people's affairs by then, wouldn't you? Not a bit of it! He apologized to the angry woman, he cleared up the mess – and then he went around looking for somebody else to meddle with.

He saw a little man, a big, plump woman, and four children all trailing along. "Oh dear, oh dear!" said the woman. "We shall miss the train, I know! Where do we get our tickets?"

"Madam, over there," said Meddle, hurrying up to her. "Shall I hold the children's hands while you get them?"

"No, thank you," said the woman. "They can hold each other's hands. Dad, get your money ready for the tickets. Oh dear, what a queue there is at the ticket-office!"

"Madam, you go and get your seats in the train, and I'll buy the tickets for you," said Meddle.

"Do go away!" said the little man, crossly. "I'm not leaving you here with my money, I wouldn't be so silly!"

"That's not a nice thing to say at all!" said Meddle, most offended. "Do you mean to say I'd run off with the money? Well, I never heard such a –"

"Do please go away," said the plump woman. "We can look after ourselves all right. Oh my, oh my, what a queue. I wish these people in front of us would hurry up, I know we shall miss our train."

"We'll catch it all right," said the little man, looking at the station clock. "But if it's crowded we shan't get any seats, that's certain."

The children began to cry. "I want a seat," sobbed one. "I want to look out of the window."

"Shall I go and get some seats for you?" said Meddle, quite determined to help in some way. "I could go and find a carriage and put newspapers and things on six seats – then no one would take those seats, and when you came along you could have them. I could hop out of the carriage and wave goodbye."

"What an extraordinary fellow!" said the little man to his wife. He turned to Meddle. "I tell you, we don't want people poking their noses into our business," he said. "We can't stop you finding seats, of course, and spreading them with newspapers and coats to keep them for us! I can see you mean to interfere with us in *some* way!"

"Not interfere – just *help*," said Meddle, quite hurt. "All right – I'm off to get some seats for you. I'll buy some newspapers to spread on them, so that people will know they are all reserved for others!"

He hurried away, pleased. He bought some papers and then ran to find the train. Bother! He had forgotten to ask which one it was. It must be the very next train leaving, because the little man and his wife were in such a hurry to get the tickets. One of the children had said they were going to the sea – now which train would it be?

"Ah – here's one leaving in five minutes – to Seaside Town," said Meddle. "This must be it. How glad they will be when they come rushing on to the platform, find the train is full – but with six seats saved for them!"

He bought a platform ticket and

hurried to the train. He found a carriage that was quite empty. Good! He sat down, and arranged four newspapers and his overcoat on five seats. He sat in the sixth himself, of course.

He felt pleased with himself. "It's so nice to help people," he said. "Now that little family will all travel comfortably to the seaside, each with a nice seat all the way."

People looked into the carriage, saw the newspapers and coat on the seats and went on again. Meddle grinned. Aha! He had been very clever, he thought.

The minutes went by. Meddle began to feel anxious. Surely those people wouldn't miss the train? He looked out of the door. There was no sign of them. Oh dear – should he go and hurry them up?

Meddle got out some pennies to buy some chocolate on his way out. One fell from his hand and rolled under the seat. Oh dear! Meddle got down. It was in the far corner. Meddle had to get halfway under the seat to reach it.

A loud whistle blew. PHEEEEEEEE! Meddle jumped. He tried to wriggle out from under the seat, but somehow or other he got stuck. "Wait, wait! Tell the engine not to go yet!" shouted Meddle, from under the seat. But nobody heard him, of course. The engine began to puff out smoke and then, with a rattle and a rumble and clatter, the train began to pull out of the station!

Meddle wriggled himself free and rushed to the window. He leaned out, shouting loudly, trying to open the door. It was a good thing he couldn't, because the train was now going quite fast.

"Stop! Stop! Let me out!" yelled Meddle. "I'm not going, I tell you!"

But he was. He couldn't help it! And the last thing that poor Meddle saw was the little man and his family all getting into a train marked 'To Golden Sands' – and finding plenty of seats, too!

"This *wasn't* their train!" groaned

poor Meddle. "And *what* will the ticket-inspector say to me if he comes and finds me without a proper ticket and all the seats to myself? Oh dear – this is what comes of helping people."

No, Meddle – that's what comes of meddling! There he goes, all the way to the sea, first stop Seaside Town.

Master Meddle and
the birds

One day when Master Meddle passed by his Aunt Jemima's, he saw that she had some new yellow canaries and some little budgies, too.

"Dear me!" said Meddle in delight. "How pretty they are! I really must go and see them!"

He popped into his aunt's house, and she came running to send him out, for she knew Meddle's interfering ways.

"Now, Meddle, out you go!" she said. "It's my washing morning and I can't have you around upsetting things and making muddles."

"Aunt Jemima, I only came in to see

your lovely new birds," said Meddle crossly. "Just let me look at them!"

"Well, take one look and go!" said his aunt. Meddle peered into the big canary-cage. There were two fine canaries there, tweeting loudly. The budgies were flying free around the room, calling to one another. They had a little perch by the window and they often flew to this to look out and see the passers-by.

"Aunt Jemima, your birds haven't very much to eat," said Meddle. "Look – only that bit of seed – and very nasty dry stuff it looks too! Why don't you feed them properly?"

"I do," said his aunt, vexed. "You don't know anything about birds, Meddle, so don't pretend you do!"

"Oh, Aunt Jemima, I know a GREAT DEAL!" said Meddle. "Birds eat worms and caterpillars and flies and grubs – they love those. Look at that canary tweeting at me with its head on one side. It knows I understand it."

"Well, you go and do a little understanding outside," said his aunt, giving him a push. "*I* know somebody who gave fish-food to Sally Simple's canary – and gave her canary seed to goldfish. Ha, ha, Meddle – that's all you know about birds."

Meddle was really very angry indeed. He walked outside in a huff without even saying good morning. But, as he went, he made up his mind to do something for his aunt's pet birds.

"Poor things! Only that dry seed to eat!" he said. "I'll collect some worms and caterpillars for them. If they were flying about like the thrushes and the blackbirds, that's what they would be feeding on! I'll take them to the birds when Aunt Jemima is out."

So Meddle began to hunt about his garden for worms and caterpillars. He had a bag for the worms and a box for the caterpillars – and, dear me, what a lot he found! He found a few beetles too, and wondered if the birds would like those as well. He put them into a tin.

Then he waited for Tuesday afternoon, when he knew Aunt Jemima went out to a sewing-meeting. He put all the things into his pocket and set off, thinking happily how pleased the birds would be to have a good meal. He crept into the kitchen of Aunt Jemima's house. Not a sound was to be heard.

"Good! She's gone already!" said Meddle, full of delight. He took out his bag of worms, his box of caterpillars, and his tin of beetles. He tiptoed into the front room.

The worms were very wriggly. Meddle found it difficult to push them through the bars of the cage. The poor worms didn't like it at all. So Meddle decided to give them to the budgies — but they were frightened of him and wouldn't come for the worms. They flew all over the room, perching on the lamp, the pictures, and the curtains.

"Oh, very well, you silly things," said Meddle crossly. "After I've taken all this trouble you might at least be pleased to see me. Well, I'll hang the worms here and there and you can get them when you like."

So Meddle draped the worms about the room — two or three on the lampshade, some on the top of the pictures, and one or two on the mantelpiece. Then he opened his box of caterpillars. They were very lively indeed.

"I'm not sure it wouldn't be a good idea to let the canaries out of their cage and let them fly round the room," said Meddle. "After all, the budgies are loose. Then I can pop the caterpillars and grubs here and there, and all the birds can share them. It will be as much fun for them as flying round my garden to find them."

It wasn't much fun for the caterpillars and worms! But Meddle didn't think of that. He put the caterpillars on the table and chairs and pictures, and he popped the beetles on the mantelpiece, where they immediately ran to hide themselves away.

The canaries were rather frightened when they were let out of their cage. They took no notice of the live food that Meddle had brought. The budgies didn't seem to want it either. Meddle was disgusted with them.

"Well, really, you might ..." he began. And then he stopped and listened in a dreadful fright.

Aunt Jemima was coming in at the front door, and with her were five friends! This Tuesday was Aunt Jemima's turn for having the sewing-meeting at her own house.

Meddle got a terrible scare. There wasn't time for him to escape. He hurriedly squeezed himself between the sofa and the wall and hid there. He did hope that the six women would not come into that room.

But they did! In they trooped all chattering merrily, and sat down. They put their sewing things on the table, and slipped their thimbles on to their fingers.

"Now, let me see, are we all here?" said Aunt Jemima. "Sally Simple, Dame Grumps, Lucy Lettuce, Mother Mangle and Fanny Fickle. Yes. Well, we can set to work at once."

Now Sally Simple was sitting just underneath the lampshade, and on it Meddle had put two or three long red worms. He watched them from his hiding-place, hoping that they wouldn't wriggle off and fall on Sally.

Suddenly one long worm wriggled too far. It fell off the silk lampshade right on to Sally's head. Sally gave a scream and put up her hand to find out what was in her hair. When she felt the long worm she squealed and squealed.

"Sally! Sally! What's the matter?" cried everyone in a fright.

"A worm dropped on me!" screamed Sally.

"Nonsense!" said Aunt Jemima. "How could a worm drop on you? Worms don't live in houses!"

A second worm dropped on Sally from the lampshade and she jumped up in fright. The third worm dropped on the table, and everybody jumped in horror.

"It *is* a worm!" said Mother Mangle. "And, oh, save us all, what's that crawling on that picture?"

Everybody looked – and they saw a big and furry caterpillar crawling on the glass. Then Dame Grumps saw two beetles running along the mantelpiece, and she squealed loudly.

A fat caterpillar dropped on to Lucy Lettuce's hand, and she yelled for help. In half a minute everyone was squealing and yelling, for they saw worms, beetles, and caterpillars everywhere. Then Aunt Jemima noticed her two frightened canaries hiding up on the top of the curtains. She hadn't noticed that they were out of their cage before.

"Jemima, this is fine state for your room to be in for a sewing-meeting!"

said Dame Grumps angrily. "I'm going! You may think it's a funny joke, but I *don't!*" She gathered up her sewing things and gave a scream — she had picked up a caterpillar too!

She jumped so much that she sent her silver thimble flying out of her hand. It dropped on Meddle, who was trembling behind the sofa. Sally Simple bent over the back of the sofa to pick up the thimble for Dame Grumps.

She saw Meddle's scared white face looking up at her, and she gave such a yell that Aunt Jemima dropped everything she was holding, and her scissors cut her foot.

"There's something behind the sofa!" yelled Sally.

"What is it? A worm? A beetle?" asked Lucy Lettuce. "Really!"

"It's some sort of horrid big insect with a white ugly face," said Sally, and she sat down, plump, in a chair and fanned herself, feeling quite faint.

Well, in another moment Meddle was

pulled out of his hiding-place, for as soon as Aunt Jemima spied him there she guessed what had happened. She shook him till his teeth rattled.

"So *you* brought all these dreadful things into my house!" she said. "Meddling again! Didn't I tell you that my birds like seed and nothing else? You take all your creatures home with you, Meddle, and don't you dare show your face in my house again unless you want a bucket of cold water all over you!"

And she stuffed all the beetles, the caterpillars, and worms down poor Meddle's neck and turned him out of doors. How he wriggled! How he shook! It was dreadful to feel things wriggling and running all over him. One by one they fell out and ran or wriggled away, very glad to be free again. They had had a most unpleasant adventure – and, dear me, so had Meddle.

"I shan't try to do a good turn again," he said in a huff. Well – we shall see!

The boy who scribbled

Bobby was a great nuisance wherever he went, because he scribbled over everything! He always took his pencils and chalks with him – and, dear me, how he scribbled on walls, seats, and pavements!

"Bobby, it is very bad manners to scribble over things like that," said his mother.

"Bobby, you've spoilt our nice new garden seat by scribbling your name all over it," said his aunt, crossly.

"Bobby, if you scribble on your desk again, you will stay in after school and write out 'I must not scribble', one hundred times," said his teacher.

But Bobby went on scribbling. You

may have seen some of his scribbles, for he scribbled everywhere. Sometimes he wrote horrid things. Once, when Ellen wouldn't lend him her book, he wrote "Ellen is a selfish girl" all over her wall in white chalk. Her mother was very angry.

The policeman was angry too, because Bobby's town tried to keep the streets clean and tidy, there were litter-bins everywhere and nobody was supposed to make a mess on the walls or fences. But Bobby simply couldn't help it.

His mother took away his chalks and his pencils. But Bobby found a sharp white stone and wrote all over the pavement with it. He was cross with George, so he wrote "George is a horrid boy" three times. George was so angry when he saw it.

Now, one day Bobby went for a picnic in a wood all by himself. He had a basket packed with goodies, and he meant to have a good time. He found a little path he hadn't seen before, and off he went into the very heart of the wood. And when he came there he found a pretty little whitewashed house, with a neat whitewashed wall around it, and bright flowers growing in the garden!

Bobby was most astonished. He stared at the house in surprise. "I didn't know anyone lived in this wood," he said to himself. "What a dear little house! I think I'll have my picnic here, and then I can go and ask for a drink of water at the house if I'm thirsty."

So he sat down nearby and undid his basket of food. There were sandwiches, cake, and apples, with a bar of chocolate to finish the meal. Bobby enjoyed it very much.

"Now for a drink!" he said. He got up and went to the little white gate. He opened it, went up the neat path, and knocked at the little white door.

But nobody came. Nobody seemed to be in the house at all. "Bother!" said Bobby. "Just when I wanted a drink!"

He went round the back to see if anyone was there. The dustbin was there, and the coal-house. A piece of coal lay on the ground. Bobby picked it up.

And then you can guess what that naughty little boy did! He began to scribble over the white walls of the cottage with the coal. He drew some little men. He drew a house with chimneys. He wrote his own name again and again – Robert William Tomkins, Robert William Tomkins.

The coal made very black lines which showed up well on the house. When Bobby had finished scribbling on the white walls, he began to scribble on the walls of the garden. He wrote "This is a silly house. There is no one to give me a drink." What a thing to do!

Then he wrote two or three things about his school friends. He put "Harry has carroty hair. Jane has rabbit-teeth. John is a cry-baby."

Just as he was finishing this, he

heard a noise. He looked up and saw six little pixie men come through the wood. They hadn't seen him, because he was sitting beside the garden wall.

Bobby felt frightened. *Six* little men! They might be very angry with him for scribbling. He looked at the house – yes, he had done a dreadful lot of scribbles there. The naughty little boy quietly picked up his basket and, bending down to hide himself behind the wall, ran off into the wood without being seen.

When the six little men came up to their house they stared in the greatest horror at their white walls, which were now all spoilt with the black coal-marks.

"Who has done this shocking thing?" said the chief little man in anger.

"Just look!" cried another. "All the way round our lovely house! Some horrid nuisance of a scribbler has been here."

"If only we knew who it was!" said the chief man. "I would punish him well!"

"I can tell you who he is," said the third little man, and he pointed to where Bobby had written his name again and again – Robert William Tomkins, Robert William Tomkins. "Look, that's his name!"

"Ha!" said the chief man, looking stern. "So that's who he is. I've heard of him before. Well, he'll be sorry for this!"

"Yes," said the little men, going to get cloths and water to wash their walls. "Yes – he'll be sorry for this!"

The little men soon found out where Bobby lived. And then one of them kept near Bobby all day long, although the boy didn't know it. The little men watched all he did. They saw him smack Nora. They saw him throw a stone at a cat. They heard him being rude to old Mrs Lucy. Oh, they soon found out quite a lot about Bobby!

And then strange things began to happen. One day when Bobby and his mother came home from a walk, they found their green front door painted

112

all over with big red letters. And this is what was written on the door – "BOBBY IS A HORRID RUDE BOY."

"Good gracious!" said his mother. "Look at that! Whoever has written that on our front door? We must get it off at once."

But they couldn't get it off, because it was painted with magic paint! So there it was for everyone to read when they went by. Bobby was angry and ashamed. He remembered that he had been rude to old Mrs Lucy, and he was careful to be polite the next time in case she had written the message!

The next thing that happened was a long message, painted in bright green on the pavement outside Bobby's house: "BOBBY IS VERY UNKIND AND SELFISH. HE HAS BIG EARS. HE IS UNKIND TO ANIMALS! HA, HA!"

"Oh dear!" said Bobby's mother, nearly in tears. "Who *can* have done that on our pavement? Bobby, how I wish you had never had that dreadful habit of scribbling over everything! Now you see what has happened! Other people are scribbling things about you too."

Bobby was red with shame. How dreadful that everyone who came by should read those things about him! He went to look at his ears. Yes – they *were* big. Well, he had teased Harry about his red hair, so perhaps it was Harry who had painted the horrid message on the pavement, and had put that Bobby had big ears.

Harry said he hadn't done anything of the sort. "I'm not a silly scribbler like you!" he cried. "All I can say is that it serves you right for being such a horrid scribbler yourself!"

The next day the nice red walls of the house were painted white with comical pictures of Bobby and his big ears. Bobby cried and cried, he was so ashamed. His mother and father went to the policeman about the scribbles, and begged for his help.

"Well, I don't feel much inclined to help that boy of yours," said the policeman. "I've had plenty of trouble from *him* over scribbling on walls and pavements, I can tell you. If you ask me, I think this just serves him right!"

But all the same the policeman kept an eye on Bobby's house that night — and when he saw six funny little men creeping up with pails and brushes, he walked up to them with a large frown.

"Now then, what's all this?" he began in a very deep voice — but to his great surprise every single one of the little men vanished! Yes, disappeared into thin air, and not even a paintbrush was left!

That was the end of the scribbling on Bobby's house. The little men came no more. Bobby's daddy had his house repainted, and the front door, too, and sent someone to clean the pavement outside. Then he spoke sternly to Bobby.

"All this has happened because of

your horrid scribbling habits," said Mr Tomkins. "Have you anything to say to me about them, Bobby?"

"I'll never scribble anywhere again, Daddy," said Bobby in a low voice. And since then he never has. I'd hate to have horrid things scribbled about me by those six little men, wouldn't you?

White trousers

The teddy bear in Jack's playroom was a fine-looking fellow. He wore a red jersey, a little blue scarf and white trousers. At least, they were white when they were new, but now they were rather dirty.

He was very proud of his clothes. "You see, only the best bears have clothes," he told everyone. "Some poor bears have no clothes at all, only their fur. But I've got very nice clothes, haven't I?"

"Yes. So you must be one of the best bears!" said Angelina, the biggest doll, with a laugh. "Come here, Teddy. You've a button off your coat! The very best bears never have buttons off."

"Oh, dear!" said the bear in alarm, squinting down at his coat with his big glass eyes. "Yes, there's a button gone. Could you sew it on, please, Angelina? You really are so good with a needle."

Angelina found the button and sewed it on. The bear gave her a furry kiss. "Ooooh," she said, "your whiskers tickle me! There! You're a nice little bear, and certainly one of the best, because you're always kind and jolly!"

All the toys loved the little bear. They belonged to Jack, a noisy, untidy boy who liked his toys but didn't bother much about them. If one broke he didn't mend it but threw it away. The toys didn't like that. They thought they should be mended if they broke.

One day something happened. It was a rainy day and Jack had to be indoors. So he got out his paints and his painting book, and filled a glass with water. He stuck his paintbrush into it and then rubbed it on one of his paints. He looked round at his toys.

"I think I'll draw one of you and paint your picture," he said. "Now, who shall it be? I think I'll have *you*, Teddy – you'll be easy to draw!"

He picked up the teddy bear and put him on the table, standing up straight. The bear was very proud and pleased. Ah, now he would have his picture painted and he would be famous!

Mummy put her head round the door. "Oh, Jack – you've got your paints out. Please be careful of that tablecloth. I told you to take it off if you wanted to do anything messy."

"Oh, Mummy, I won't spill anything. I'll be careful!" said Jack, impatiently.

He drew the little bear, white trousers and all. Then he picked up his paintbrush again, rubbed it on this paint and that, and began to splash the colours on to the paper. How the bear wished he could see the picture! And then Jack moved his hand too quickly and knocked the glass of painting-water over on the tablecloth!

"Bother!" said Jack, staring at the coloured pool of water. "I must wipe it up before Mummy comes in. But what with?"

There was no cloth or duster in the room. Jack could hear his mother in the next room, and he looked wildly round for something to wipe up the mess. He suddenly grabbed the bear.

"I'll have your white trousers!" he said. And, oh dear, he tore them off the surprised little bear! He mopped up the pool of water with the thick trousers, and then covered the wet patch with his painting book. Now Mummy wouldn't know!

The bear was full of dismay. His trousers, his lovely white trousers! They had been used to mop up that water — and oh, goodness gracious, Jack had now thrown them into the fire! They burned slowly for they were damp. The bear sat down suddenly on the table, feeling quite sad.

When Jack had gone down to his tea

the bear climbed down miserably. The toys clustered round him.

"You look peculiar," said the pink rabbit. "Hadn't you better take off your coat and tie? It looks odd to wear those and no trousers."

"No, no. Let me keep my coat and tie," said the bear, holding on to them as if he thought the toys were going to take them off. "Oh, dear – my nice white trousers! Jack threw them in the fire, all wet and messy – and they've *burrrrnnnt!*"

He began to cry. The toys tried to comfort him. "It's a shame," said the pink cat. "He must feel cold without his white trousers."

"Oh, I do, I do," wept the bear. "And I'm not one of the best bears any more because I'm only half-dressed. I shall never be happy again!"

"It was mean of Jack," said Angelina, beginning to think hard. "He's a naughty boy. He does lots of things that his mother doesn't guess. For instance, she thinks he cleans his teeth night and morning and washes his neck and behind his ears with his flannel. But he doesn't."

"He *never* uses his flannel!" said the pink rabbit. "He only just splashes water on his face."

Angelina suddenly looked at the pink rabbit. "I've got an idea," she said. "Quite a good one. Why shouldn't we get Jack's white flannel and make the bear a pair of white trousers out of it? Jack never uses the flannel, so it won't matter!"

"Oh, Angelina, please, please do!" begged the bear and kissed her so that his whiskers tickled her again. "Oh, Angelina, you're the cleverest doll in the world!"

Angelina laughed. She sent the pink rabbit to climb up to Jack's basin and fetch the white flannel. It was quite dry because Jack never used it. He put it down beside Angelina. She took the pair of scissors that Jack used to cut his nails, and she began to cut the flannel!

All the toys watched her. How clever Angelina was! Snip, snip, snip, snippety, snip!

"There's one leg," said Angelina, "and there's another. And this bit is to go round his tummy, and that is for his back. My, Bear, you're going to look fine!"

It really was exciting to see Angelina make those white trousers. She sewed away with her needle, she sent Rabbit to get a button from Mummy's work-basket, and she made a nice buttonhole, so that the white trousers did up tightly.

"There!" she said. "They're finished. Try them on, Teddy dear!" So the bear tried them on, putting first one fat leg into them and then the other. He pulled them up and buttoned them. Then he walked proudly about in front of the toys.

"Perfect!" said the pink rabbit.

"They fit him beautifully!" said the toy cat. "I wouldn't mind a pair like that myself, though I suppose I'd have to have two pairs for my four legs."

"You look sweet," said Angelina, laughing. "Face-flannel trousers! Who would have thought they could look so fine? You certainly are one of the Best Bears again now!"

"What *I'm* wondering," said the pink rabbit, "what *I'm* wondering is – what will Jack say when his mother asks him how he manages to wash himself properly without his face flannel?"

"He'll have to own up for once!" said Angelina. "He'll have to say it's disappeared and he hasn't *been* washing himself!"

"Oh, I'm so happy!" sang the little bear, walking up and down. "Look at my white trousers, everyone, do look!"

So they looked – and I'd have liked to look, too. Face-flannel trousers – well, well, well!

The tale of Tinker the pup

I am a puppy dog, and my name is Tinker. I am in disgrace, and I have been put in the corner; it is a great shame.

"Tinker," my mistress said, "you have been a very naughty little dog all day long! I am ashamed of you!"

Well *I* don't think I have been at all naughty, and I am just going to tell you all I have done today, then you will know that my mistress is quite mistaken. I am a very good dog.

I woke up at six o'clock, and got out of my basket. I sleep with my master and mistress, and my basket is put in the corner of their bedroom. I felt a bit lonely, so I jumped up on the bed.

The eiderdown tickled my nose, so I bit a big hole in it, the nasty thing – and oh, do you know, it was full of the most exciting little feathers! They all came blowing out when I breathed on them. So I spent a lovely time chasing them, and biting them. I thought my mistress would be pleased when she woke up and saw how many I had caught.

But she wasn't! No, not a bit! She was *ever* so cross! She said I had spoilt her eiderdown.

So I went downstairs to the cook. She was pleased to see me, and gave me a pat and a biscuit. I licked her hand, and then tried to fight her feet, but she wouldn't let me.

Soon I found a scrubbing-brush on the floor, and didn't I have a game with it! I had torn all the bristles out before Cook found me.

"That was a fine brush you put down for me to play with," I said to her. But would you believe it, she was very angry.

"You wicked little dog!" she said. "Fancy ruining a lovely new brush like that!"

After breakfast I went upstairs to sniff round the bedrooms. I found a nice soft slipper under my master's bed. So I pulled it out, and looked at it.

"Play with me!" I said. But it wouldn't. No matter how much I asked it to, it wouldn't play at all. I thought it was very horrid of it, and I gave it a bite just to show it what I thought. But still it wouldn't play.

Then I got really fierce and shook it hard between my teeth. "I'll teach you not to play with me, you horrid, impolite thing!" I said.

I did teach it. It was all in bits before I had finished, and I'm sure it was very sorry it had been so horrid to me. Then – oh, dear! – my mistress came along.

"My lovely bedroom slipper!" she cried. "Oh, you bad little puppy! You've nibbled it all to bits!"

I tried to tell my mistress that that

was a good punishment for impolite slippers, but she wouldn't listen. She took me by the scruff of my neck and dragged me downstairs.

"I'll smack you the very next time you are naughty today!" she said, and she shut me into the kitchen.

Well, no sooner had I got there, than I smelt the *loveliest* smell I have ever smelt. It was SAUSAGES.

There was a long string of them on the table.

"I expect Cook has brought one for me," I said to myself. "Well, I'm hungry, so I'll have it now."

I took the end one into my mouth – but they were all joined together, so the whole string fell down on to the floor.

"I'd better take my sausage into the yard in case Cook remembers about the scrubbing brush," I thought. So I tried to drag my one sausage into the backyard – but all the other sausages came too. I couldn't make them stop coming.

"Well, if you *really* must come," I said. "I warn you, you may be eaten."

I thought that would make them scurry away – but it didn't. So I ate them all, every one. Weren't they lovely!

But oh, Cook was crosser than ever I've seen her before. She took up a broom and chased me with it. I scuttled out into the garden as fast as I could go.

"What horrid people live in my house!" I thought to myself. "I've a good mind not to live here any more."

Just then I heard a funny sort of noise, and in the next garden I saw a lot of fluffy yellow chicks. They were cheeping loudly, and making such a noise.

"Be quiet," I growled. "I have a headache, and I want to go to sleep."

Well, those disobedient little chicks wouldn't take a bit of notice of me, so I squeezed my way through the hedge and went to tell them what I thought of them.

I ran at them, and they all scurried away, cheeping loudly. I thought this was rather a nice game, so I chased them all over the place. And then – my goodness – the fiercest old hen came up and was *ever* so rude to me.

She flew at me, and pecked me on the nose three times. I couldn't seem to get away from her. But at last I did, and I squeezed through the hedge as quick as anything, with that horrid old hen pecking me all the time.

"It's no wonder your chicks are bad-mannered if they've got a mother like you!" I said. Then I ran up the garden as fast as I could.

I hadn't gone very far when I remembered that I had buried a bone somewhere yesterday. So I began to look for it. There were a lot of those red, blue, and yellow things about – flowers, my mistress calls them – and they were in my way. So I scraped a whole lot up, but still I couldn't find my bone.

Then I suddenly remembered where I

had buried it, and I ran to the bed. The gardener had put dozens of little green plants in it – just like him to use my bone-bed for that – so I had to dig them all up.

It was just whilst I was doing that – and making a very good job of it too – that my master came out and saw me.

"You young rascal!" he said. Then he carried me indoors to my mistress.

"He's dug up half the garden," said Master. "Put him in the corner, and tie him up for the rest of the day, my dear. He'll dig up the house next."

So here I am in the corner, and nobody will speak to me because I am in disgrace. But *I* don't think I have been so very bad, do you?

Sneezing powder

Once upon a time there lived a brownie called Smarty. He kept a little shop in Hallo Town, in which he sold jars of honey, fine yellow lemons, and big yellow pills that helped to cure colds.

In the winter-time Smarty did a fine trade, for anyone who had a cold came to buy his honey, his juicy lemons, and his cold-pills. Then they would go home, squeeze the lemons into a glass, put in hot water and sugar and a spoonful or two of Smarty's golden honey, take a cold-pill, and go to bed — and lo and behold, next morning they were cured!

But in the summer-time nobody seemed to have a cold at all. It was most annoying for Smarty. Instead of thinking of selling something else, such as ice-creams or cool lemon drinks, Smarty still went on hoping that people would have colds and buy his cold-cure. So he wasn't quite as smart as his name, was he?

He was quite smart enough to think out a naughty trick, though!

"If only I could *make* people think they had a cold, they would come and buy my honey and lemons and pills," thought Smarty. "If only they would sneeze or cough just as they passed my shop, it would be so easy for me to say, 'Dear me! You are getting a cold! Buy my cold-cure before you are very bad!' But nobody ever sneezes outside my shop."

Smarty sat and thought for a bit, and then he grinned all over his sly little face. He slapped his knee in delight. He had thought of a wonderful idea!

"I'll go and buy some sneezing powder from old Dame Flap!" he said to himself.

"And I'll put some into my pepper-pot and shake it out of my bedroom window whenever anyone passes! Then they will sneeze hard, and perhaps come and buy my goods."

So off he went to buy the sneezing powder. He paid Dame Flap a silver coin for a boxful and she wrapped it up for him. It was a strange powder, rather like fine green flour, and it had a strange smell.

Smarty ran home with it. He emptied some into his pepper-pot and slipped upstairs to his bedroom window, which was just over his shop. He leaned out in excitement. Was anybody coming?

Yes – here was Old Man Shuffle! Smarty waited till he was underneath the window and then he shook out some of the powder. It went on Old Man Shuffle's nose, and he stopped. He took out his big blue handkerchief and held it to his nose.

"Whooosh!" he sneezed. "A-whoosh!"

"Hi, Old Man Shuffle, you've got a

dreadful cold!" called Smarty. "Come into my shop and get some honey and lemons and pills!"

So in shuffled the old fellow, thinking it was very lucky that he should be outside Smarty's shop just when his cold had begun. He bought a jar of honey, two lemons, and a box of yellow pills. Smarty grinned. He ran up to his bedroom again.

"Ah! Here are Mr Twiddle and his wife!" chuckled Smarty. He shook his pepper-pot over them. They stopped and fumbled for their hankies.

"Er-tish-oo!" said Mr Twiddle loudly.

"Ish-ish-ish!" sneezed Mrs Twiddle politely into her handkerchief.

"ER-TISH-OOO!" went Mr Twiddle.

"Not so much noise, Twiddle," said Mrs Twiddle. "Ish-ish-ish-ish! Dear me! We are beginning colds, I think. Look, let's buy some honey and lemons, and maybe we'll stop our colds from getting worse."

So into Smarty's shop they went and

bought what they wanted, much to Smarty's delight. As soon as they had gone, he popped upstairs again with his pepper-pot full of sneezing powder.

He made Twinkle the pixie sneeze and buy honey and pills. He made Mr Meddle sneeze so strongly that his hat flew on to the roof and he had to get a ladder to fetch it. He made Dame Winks sneeze twelve times, and at the end her bonnet was right over her nose and she couldn't see where she was going at all.

Oh, Smarty had plenty of fun that day, and he made plenty of money, too! But when everyone found that they had no cold at all when they got home, and didn't need the honey and lemons, they were rather puzzled. They talked about it to one another, and they found that all of them had begun their sneezing fits outside Smarty's shop.

"Very nice for Smarty!" said Mr Meddle. "Let us go along and see what we can see."

So they all went back towards Smarty's shop, and peeped round the corner. And they saw Smarty leaning out of his bedroom window, pepper-pot in hand!

"Aha!" said Old Man Shuffle angrily. "So that's his trick, is it! Come along, everybody!"

They all went into Smarty's shop. Smarty hurried down to serve them. Mrs Twiddle was waiting for him. She snatched the pepper-pot out of his pocket and shook it all over Smarty.

"Colds are catching today!" she said. "Sneeze, Smarty, sneeze! Dear, dear! You must have caught our colds."

"Whoosh!" said Smarty. "Atish-oo! Ish-ish-ish! Osha-whoosh! Tish-oo!"

Mrs Twiddle emptied all the sneezing powder over him. My goodness, Smarty simply could *not* stop sneezing! It was dreadful!

"By the time you've finished I guess you'll want to buy a pot of your own honey, a dozen lemons, and a box of pills!" said Mr Twiddle, laughing. "Goodbye, Smarty. It serves you right!"

They all went out, giggling and chuckling, and they could hear Smarty's sneezes all the way down the road.

Poor Smarty! He sneezed all that day and all that night, and by that time his nose and throat and eyes were so sore that he had to take two jars of honey, six lemons, and two of his own pills to cure himself!

Now he has shut up his shop and gone out selling ice-creams. And a very much better idea, too, in the summer – don't you think so?

Trundle goes out to tea

If ever you go to the little brownie village of Tucked-Away you will notice a curious thing. You will see that every brownie wears a green leaf sewn into his tight little breeches, just over his right knee-cap. And you are sure to wonder why.

Well, I will tell you the reason, because I'm sure you won't like to ask the brownies. We shall have to go right back to the day when Trundle the brownie went out to tea.

Now Trundle didn't live in the village of Tucked-Away. Oh dear me no, *he* lived in the town of Very-Big, where everything was up-to-date, and all the brownies wore the very latest thing in pointed caps, and knew exactly how many buttons should go on a coat, and important things like that.

The brownies of Tucked-Away were very old-fashioned, although they tried hard not to be. As Trundle said, they simply did not *know* how to dress. They wore fifteen buttons down their coats when everyone in Very-Big was only wearing fourteen, and had five pockets instead of two.

The village of Tucked-Away thought a lot of Very-Big, and whenever a visitor from the town paid them a visit they were very much excited. They made everything as nice as ever they could and tried their hardest to show the visitor that they could do things quite as well as Very-Big.

So you can imagine that when Trundle said he would go and have tea with his cousin in Tucked-Away there was great excitement. Trundle was a very up-to-date brownie, and always dressed just so. Jinks, his cousin, couldn't keep the news to himself when he got Trundle's letter, and he rushed round to all his friends to tell them that a brownie from Very-Big was coming to tea the very next Friday.

"I'll have a tea-party," he said, "and you must all come, dressed in your very best things, and we'll show Trundle that the village of Tucked-Away can be just as well dressed as the town of Very-Big!"

So everyone began to take out best suits and sponge them and iron them. They polished up the buttons, and put clean handkerchiefs in the breast pockets all ready for the tea-party.

Jinks made all sorts of scones and cakes and bought three different sorts of jam from the jam-woman. He made a yellow jelly and a red one, and when the day came you should have seen his tea-table. It was enough to make your mouth water! The brownies going by his cottage in the morning peeped in through the window, and what they

143

saw made them long for the afternoon to come.

Jinks had asked everybody to come at four o'clock. Trundle was coming at half-past three, and Jinks thought that his visitor would just have time to wash and polish up his shoes before all the guests came.

At half-past two Trundle started out from the town of Very-Big to walk to Tucked-Away, which was four miles away. He had on his newest suit, and a fine new hat with a red feather in it. He liked his cousin Jinks and he was looking forward to the tea-party, for he hadn't had much dinner.

He went merrily along, whistling a tune, walking in the shade, for the sun was hot. He was very nearly at Tucked-Away when a dreadful thing happened. Trundle caught his foot on a root and tumbled right over! And when he got up again, he found that he had torn a big hole in his nice red breeches, just over his right knee-cap!

"Oh, my!" said Trundle, in dismay. "Now isn't that unfortunate? Never mind, Jinks is sure to offer me a needle and thread when I get to his house, and I'll just have to mend it up as best I can."

He took a green leaf, and tucked it into the hole, for his knee was grazed and bleeding a little, and he didn't want his socks to be stained. Then he went on his way again, and soon arrived at Jinks' little cottage.

Jinks was at the door to greet him, and took him indoors to wash after his dusty walk. Jinks looked at his cousin's suit carefully, and decided that his own was just as fashionable – and then he caught sight of the green leaf stuck over Trundle's knee-cap.

"Dear me!" he thought. "*That's* a new idea, surely! I suppose it's a sort of trimming. Dear, dear, dear, and not one of my guests will be in the fashion now, for none of us has got green-leaf trimming on his right knee! What can I do? There's half an hour before the tea-party begins, so perhaps there's just time to send little notes round and tell everyone to wear a green leaf sewn on to their right knee."

"The guests won't be here for a little while, Trundle," said Jinks to his visitor. "Would you like to go and sit out in the garden, and rest after your long walk?"

So whilst Trundle was resting in the garden, Jinks hurriedly wrote lots of little notes, and gave them to his servant to deliver.

"Please be sure to wear a green leaf as trimming, sewn over your right knee-cap," said each note. "It is the latest fashion in Very-Big. Trundle is wearing one this afternoon."

You can guess that when the guests received these notes they all rushed out in a great hurry, and got green leaves to sew on to their right knee-caps. That took time, so they were all a bit late when they arrived.

Trundle fell fast asleep in the garden,

and when he awoke he saw the first of the guests coming in at the gate.

"My goodness!" he cried. "I haven't mended this hole in the knee of my breeches! Whatever will the guests think of me?"

He got up to go and shake hands with the little brownie coming into the garden. When he saw the first one, he was very much astonished.

"What an extraordinary thing!" he thought. "Here's another brownie who must have tumbled down and torn his suit too, because he's got a green leaf over his knee-cap like me!"

His astonishment was even greater when he saw that the second brownie had a green leaf over his knee as well. And the third one, and the fourth! *And* his cousin, who certainly hadn't when he had met him at the door!

"Bless us, they've *all* got green leaves on their knees!" thought Trundle in the greatest amazement. "Am I in a dream, or what?"

He thought he really couldn't be, for the cakes tasted just like real ones, and as for the jelly, it was simply lovely. All the brownies seemed so very pleased with themselves, and looked proudly, first at Trundle's leaf-trimmed knee and then at their own.

Trundle was more and more puzzled, until a little brownie suddenly helped him to solve the mystery.

"Such a pretty new fashion, the leaf-trimming on the knee, isn't it?" said the brownie to Trundle. "As you see, Tucked-Away is not behind Very-Big in fashion!"

"*Well!*" thought Trundle. "Why in the world do they think that there's a fashion of that sort in Very-Big? There certainly isn't and never will be! I wonder – I wonder – is it possible that Jinks thought I was wearing this leaf as a sort of trimming and didn't guess I'd tumbled down and torn my breeches? He certainly didn't offer me a needle and thread to mend it with as I thought he would. I suppose he sent round notes to all the guests to tell them to wear leaves too, so as to be in the fashion! Oh, dear me, what a joke!"

Trundle had guessed quite rightly, and it made him smile to look round the tea-party and see everyone proudly wearing leaves over their right knees, thinking that they were very fashionable indeed.

"I mustn't let them know that there's no such fashion," he thought. "They would be so terribly upset – but, oh dear, if this isn't the very funniest thing that ever I saw!"

Trundle tried his hardest not to laugh, for he was a kind-hearted little brownie, but for once in a way he was quite glad when the party came to an end. He wanted to laugh and laugh!

And all the way home he *did* laugh! You should just have heard him! Even the bunnies peeped out of their holes and laughed too, although they didn't know why!

From that day to this the village of Tucked-Away has kept to the fashion — so if ever you meet a brownie wearing a green leaf on his right knee, you will know where he comes from!

The cuckoo in the clock

In the playroom on the wall hung a cuckoo clock. Every hour the little wooden cuckoo sprang out of the little door at the top and called "Cuckoo!" very loudly indeed. Then it went back into its tiny room inside the clock and stayed there all by itself until the next hour came.

The wooden cuckoo was very lonely. There was nothing to do inside the clock except look at all the wheels going round, and he was tired of that. He was a most intelligent little cuckoo, and when the children talked near the clock, he listened to every word, and learnt quite a lot.

He knew when the bluebells were out

in the wood, for he had heard Lulu say that she was going bluebelling. And he knew that seven times six are forty-two, because once Barbara had to say it twelve times running because she hadn't learnt it properly the day before.

So you see he was quite a wise little cuckoo, considering that he lived in a tiny room inside a clock all day long. He knew many things, and he longed to talk to someone in the big world outside.

But nobody ever came to see him. The children had heard him cuckoo so often that they didn't think anything about him, and except when the clock was dusted each morning nobody came near him at all.

And then one night a wonderful thing happened. The little fairy Pitapat asked all the toys in the toy cupboard to a party at midnight! What excitement there was!

The teddy bear, the sailor doll and the baby doll all got themselves as clean and smart as could be. The wooden

Dutch doll scrubbed her rosy face clean, and the Japanese doll tied her sash in a pretty bow. The soldiers marched out of their box, and just as midnight came, the fairy Pitapat flew in at the window!

The cuckoo had to pop out at that moment to cuckoo twelve times, so he had a fine view of everything. He thought that Pitapat looked the dearest little fairy in the world – and then, dear me, his heart nearly stood still!

For Pitapat looked up at the clock, and saw him! She laughed and said: "Oh, what a lovely little cuckoo! And what a beautiful voice he has! I must ask him to come to my party."

She flew up to the clock, and asked the cuckoo to come to the party. He trembled with delight, and said yes, he would love to come. So down he flew among the toys and soon he was quite at home with them.

The party was in full swing and everyone was having a lovely time, when suddenly the door was slowly pushed open. Pitapat saw it first and she gave a little scream of fright.

"Quick!" she said. "Someone's coming! Back to your cupboard, all you toys!"

The toys scuttled back to the cupboard as fast as could be, just as Whiskers, the big black cat, put his head round the door. He saw something moving and made a pounce! And oh my, he caught poor little Pitapat, who was just going to fly away out of the window.

The cuckoo had flown safely up to his little room in the clock, and he peeped out when he heard Pitapat cry out. When he saw that Whiskers had got her, he didn't know *what* to do! He was terrified of cats – but he simply couldn't bear to think that Pitapat was in danger, with no one to help her at all.

So with a very loud "Cuckoo" indeed he flew bravely down to the floor. With his wooden beak he caught hold of Whiskers' tail and pulled and pulled and pulled. Whiskers couldn't think what it was that was tugging so hard at his tail, and he looked round to see.

In a trice the cuckoo flew to Pitapat, and picked her up in his claws. He flew to his clock, and, very much out of breath, put the little fairy down just inside his tiny room. Whiskers gave a mew of disgust when he found that the fairy had gone, and jumped out of the window.

The moon sent a ray of light to the cuckoo, and he could see Pitapat quite plainly. She looked very ill, and was as white as a snowdrop. The cuckoo felt certain that she ought to be in bed. But there was no bed in his little room!

Then he suddenly thought of the tiny bed in the small dolls' house in the toy cupboard. He flew down and asked the sailor doll to get it out for him. It was not long before he had the little bed in his beak, and was flying with it back to the clock.

He popped Pitapat into bed, and then fetched her a cup of milk from the dolls' house larder. She said she felt much better, and thanked him. Then she put her golden head down on the pillow and fell fast asleep. How pleased the cuckoo was that he had rescued her! He thought that she really was the loveliest little creature that he had ever seen.

For a whole week she stayed with him, and they talked and laughed together merrily. The cuckoo felt very sad when the week drew near to an end, for he really didn't know *what* he would do without his tiny friend. He knew that he would be lonelier than ever.

Then a wonderful idea came to him. If only Pitapat would marry him, they could live together always and he wouldn't be lonely any more! But would a fairy like to live in a tiny room inside a clock with a funny old wooden cuckoo? The cuckoo shook his head, and felt certain that she wouldn't. And a big tear came into one of his eyes and rolled down his beak.

Pitapat saw it, and ran to him. She put her arms round his neck and begged him to tell her why he was sad.

"I am sad and unhappy because soon you will go away, and I shall be all alone again," said the cuckoo. "I love you very much, Pitapat, and I wish I wasn't an ugly old wooden cuckoo with a stupid cuckooing voice, living in a tiny room inside a clock. Perhaps if I were a beautiful robin or a singing thrush you would marry me and we would live happily ever after."

"You aren't ugly and old!" cried the fairy, "and your voice is the loveliest I have ever heard! You are nicer than any robin or thrush, for you are the kindest bird I have ever met! And I will marry you tomorrow, and live with you in your clock!"

Well, the cuckoo could hardly believe in his good fortune! They asked all the toys to a wedding party, and Pitapat bought the cuckoo a blue bow to wear round his neck so that he looked very grand indeed. And after the party they went back to the clock and danced a happy jig together round the little room.

"I can make this room lovely!" said the fairy happily. "I will have blue curtains at the windows, and a tiny pot of geraniums underneath. I will get some little red chairs and a tiny table to match. Oh, we will have a lovely little house here, Cuckoo!"

She set to work, and she made the dearest little place you ever saw. The cuckoo loved it, and one day when Pitapat had brought a new blue carpet and put it down, he was so pleased that he quite forgot to spring out of his door at ten o'clock and cuckoo!

There was no one in the playroom but Barbara, and she was most surprised to find that the cuckoo didn't come out and cuckoo. She got a chair and put it under the clock. Then she stood on it and opened the little door.

And, to her very great surprise and delight, she saw Pitapat's little room, so bright and pretty, and the cuckoo and Pitapat sitting down to a cup of cocoa and a biscuit each! Weren't they surprised to see their door open and Barbara's two big eyes looking in!

"Don't tell our secret, Barbara dear!" cried Pitapat. "We are so happy. *Don't* tell our secret! Please! Please!"

"I'll keep your secret," promised Barbara. "But please do let me peep into your dear little house each day. It is so little and lovely."

"You can do that and welcome," said the cuckoo, and he got up and bowed.

So every day when there is no one in the playroom Barbara peeps into the cuckoo's home in the clock; and you will be glad to know that she has kept her word – she hasn't told a single soul the secret!

The wallpaper bunnies

On the playroom wall was a lovely wallpaper. It had bunnies all over it. They were nice bunnies, all dressed up in coats and dresses and shawls, and they were doing all kinds of things. Some were shopping, and some were gardening, and some were putting their children to bed.

Ellen and Harry, the two children whose playroom it was, loved their wallpaper. They liked seeing all the bunnies on it, and they knew them very well.

"That's Mrs Flop Bunny going shopping," said Ellen. "And that's Mr Whiskers Bunny who's gardening."

"And that's Mr Woffle Bunny who's

helping him," said Harry. "And those children are the Bobtail Bunnies. I wish they'd all come alive!"

Now the wallpaper bunnies heard the children say this, and at once they began to worry about coming alive. The toys came alive each night. The kitten that played in the playroom was very much alive, and so was Pongo, the dog. Well, why shouldn't the bunnies come alive, too?

So that night, when the toys were all alive-oh, playing catch-me and hide-and-seek in the playroom, the wallpaper bunnies called down to them from the wall.

"Hi, you toys! We want to come alive too!"

The toys stopped their playing and stared at the wallpaper bunnies in surprise. This was the first time they had heard them speak.

"But you can't come alive," they said. "You are only paper."

"Well, what does that matter?" said

Mrs Flop Bunny, from the paper greengrocer's shop! "We can come alive even if we're only paper, can't we? Some of you are only rag and sawdust, but you're alive and kicking!"

"But we don't know how to make you come alive," said the red-haired doll.

"Oh dear! Don't you? Well, we did think that clever toys like you would know how to do that," sighed Mr Woffle Bunny.

The red-haired doll thought hard. Then she spoke to the teddy bear, who nodded his head.

"Well," said the doll, "there's only one thing that I can think of – and that is, we can do what Ellen and Harry do to their paper dolls. We can cut you out of the paper and stand you up! How would you like that?"

"A splendid idea, a truly fine idea!" cried all the wallpaper bunnies, and if they could have moved, they would have danced in delight. But they couldn't.

"I'll borrow the scissors out of the work-basket," said the red-haired doll, getting rather excited.

"Well, mind you put them back, then," said the clockwork clown. "You know how cross Ellen was when I borrowed her thimble for a hat the other night, and forgot to put it back."

The doll went to the work-basket on the chair and opened it. She took out the scissors. She ran over to the wallpaper.

"Snip-snip-snippity-snip!" went her scissors. "Snip-snip-snippity-snip!"

She cut out Mrs Flop Bunny, and her shopping basket too. She cut out Mr Whiskers Bunny and his spade, and Mr Woffle Bunny and his barrow. And she cut out six little Bobtail Bunnies with their hats and shoes and dresses! Really, you should have seen them all!

They hopped down to the playroom floor and scampered about joyfully. What fun it was to be alive!

"I shall do some real shopping!" said Mrs Flop Bunny, and she went to the toy greengrocer's shop that belonged to Harry, and asked the shopman there for three carrots. He put them into her basket, and she was so pleased.

"And I shall really go gardening!" said Mr Whiskers Bunny, and he climbed all the way up the tablecloth with Mr Woffle Bunny and began to dig in the pot of bulbs there! Goodness, wasn't he pleased to see his spade getting nice and earthy! As for Mr Woffle Bunny, he filled his little barrow with real earth and thoroughly enjoyed himself. His barrow felt heavy for the first time.

The Bobtail Bunnies were very frisky. They were only baby bunnies, so they didn't do any work. They just ran about among the toys, who made a great fuss of them.

"Here's a bead necklace for you," said the red-haired doll to a little Bobtail Bunny. She slipped it round the little thing's neck.

"And here's a flower for you," said the teddy bear, taking a daisy out of a vase near by, and giving it to another little Bobtail.

"And here's a brooch for you!" said the clockwork clown, pinning a brooch on to another Bobtail Bunny. The brooch had come out of a cracker, and it was very beautiful.

Well, all the little Bobtail family had presents, and they were all as happy as could be – until something nasty happened.

The Noah's Ark animals had all come out to play – and suddenly the two foxes who lived there saw the wallpaper bunnies! Their eyes gleamed! Rabbits! Aha! They had never had a meal of rabbits – and now here were ever so many scampering all over the playroom!

One Noah's Ark fox hid behind the chair, hoping that a Bobtail Bunny would come by. The other one hid behind the stool.

The toys saw them, and wondered what they were doing. Suddenly the clockwork clown guessed, and he squealed out to the bunnies, "Be careful! The Noah's Ark foxes are out! They may catch you!"

Well, this was a terrible shock to the wallpaper bunnies. There had been no foxes in their wallpaper world, so they really didn't know anything about foxes at all.

Mrs Flop Bunny at once called the Bobtail Bunnies to her, and glared at the fox behind the stool. She could just see his tail.

"How dare you!" she cried. "I won't have you catching the Bobtail children!"

Mr Whiskers Bunny was most alarmed. He put his spade over his shoulder and ran to join Mrs Flop Bunny. As for Mr Woffle Bunny, he tripped over himself and sat down in his barrow of earth! Then, very quickly, he wheeled it off and joined the other bunnies.

The two foxes came out from behind the stool and the chair and stared at the bunnies, their eyes shining, for they were hungry.

"You are *not* to eat the wallpaper bunnies!" said the teddy bear crossly. "Leave them alone."

"We are only made of paper," said Mrs Flop Bunny in a trembling voice. "You would not find us much of a meal. We should probably make you very ill."

"We are really very thin indeed," said Mr Whiskers Bunny, and he turned himself sideways to the foxes, so that they could see he really was as thin as paper. "We may look fat from the front and back, but if you see us sideways we are very narrow indeed."

Just then there was a noise outside the playroom door, and the toys looked alarmed. All the Noah's Ark animals ran to hide, and so did the toys. The Noah's Ark animals hadn't time to get back into the Ark, so some hid in one place and some in another. The two foxes went to hide in the empty brick-box.

Well, it was only a mouse scampering by, after all, so the toys soon got over their fright. Then the clown did something very clever indeed. He ran to the brick-box and put a heavy book on top of it. Now the two foxes inside couldn't get out!

How angry they were! They scrambled round inside that box as if they were chasing bees! But they couldn't get out.

"They're safe for the moment," said the red-haired doll. "But if Ellen or Harry lets them out tomorrow, they'll be after you again the next night, Wallpaper Bunnies. Whatever will you do?"

"It was a great mistake leaving our safe Wallpaper Land," said Mrs Flop Bunny. "There are no foxes there."

"Well, you'd better go back," said the teddy bear.

"We can't," said Mr Whiskers Bunny sorrowfully. "We should fall off the wall if we tried to put ourselves back."

"I know a good idea!" cried the red-haired doll, who really was good at thinking of things. "Where's the glue? You know – that sticky stuff that Ellen uses to stick us together again when we get broken? We could stick the wallpaper bunnies back on the wall again, and nobody would ever know they had left it."

Everybody began to look for the glue. At last it was found. It was in a long tube, and when the teddy bear squeezed one end the glue came out at the other in a sticky worm. It was quite exciting to play with.

The red-haired doll squeezed a little on to the back of every wallpaper bunny. They each took a running jump at the wall, and landed back in their places. The teddy bear fitted them in properly, and the clown smoothed them over with a duster.

Soon they were all back in Wallpaper Land as happy as could be.

"No one will ever know we've been

alive for just one night!" cried Mrs Flop Bunny.

But, you know, Ellen and Harry guessed they had – and do you know why? It was because Mrs Flop Bunny had forgotten to leave behind the three carrots she had put into her basket, which had been empty before! And Mr Whiskers Bunny had forgotten to clean his spade, so it was all dirty; and Mr Woffle Bunny had forgotten to empty out his earth – and as his barrow had been empty before, Ellen and Harry were most puzzled to find it full the next morning!

All the Bobtail Bunnies had their presents with them too, and the children knew quite well they had not worn necklaces and brooches before. It was very mysterious!

"Well, all I can say is that some of the wallpaper bunnies have come alive at some time," said Ellen. "And that's why this little lot look different from how they always used to be. I do wonder why they went back to the wallpaper instead of staying alive?"

They've only got to ask the Noah's Ark foxes and they'll know the reason, won't they?

Miss Waddle-Toes

Once upon a time there was a little girl called Anna. She lived in a big house with a very big garden. She was a dear, pretty little girl – except when she walked! And dear me, when she walked, *how* she turned in her toes!

"I shall call you Miss Waddle-Toes," said her mother. "You walk like a duck, Anna. It looks dreadful. Do turn your feet out, not in!"

But Anna wouldn't bother to remember to turn out her toes properly. She turned them in as much as ever, and only laughed when Mummy called her Miss Waddle-Toes.

Now one day Anna had a great surprise. She found a tiny fairy caught in a spider's web, crying loudly for help. The little girl tore the web, frightened away the big spider there, and set the small fairy on the ground.

"You are very kind," said the fairy gratefully. "What can I do for you in return?"

Anna was excited.

"Please," she said, "I have always wanted to go to a fairy party. Do you think I could?"

"Yes," said the fairy at once. "There is a dance tonight under the big oak tree at the bottom of your garden. But it's fancy dress."

"Oh dear!" said Anna. "I haven't a fancy dress, I'm afraid."

"Well, come anyhow," said the fairy. "We can dress you up somehow, I expect!"

So Anna ran inside, feeling so excited that her mother really could *not* think what was the matter with her!

That night, when the moon rose high in the starry sky, Anna slipped out of bed and ran to the window. Yes – it must be time to go to the party, because she could see tiny lights gleaming here and there at the bottom of the garden. Oh, what fun!

The little girl slipped on her dressing-gown, ran downstairs, let herself quietly out of the garden door, and ran down to the bottom of the garden.

The party had begun! The garden was lit with tiny lanterns, and hundreds of pixies, elves, brownies, and gnomes were there, all in fancy dress, talking in high twittering voices, and dancing round and round with each other.

"Hello!" cried a voice, and a gnome danced up to her. "Here comes Miss Waddle-Toes, with her toes turned in as usual! Have you come to the party?"

"Yes," said Anna. "The fairy I saved from a spider today said I could come."

"Well, you must have a fancy dress," said the gnome, "and you must be made smaller, or you won't be able to dance with us. Wait till I get my wand, then

I'll give you some kind of fancy dress."

He ran off and fetched a tiny silver wand with a glittering star on the end. He looked at Anna.

"I don't know what sort of fancy dress will come when I touch you with my wand," he said. "You don't mind, do you?"

"Not at all," said Anna, hoping very much she would have a fairy's dress or perhaps a brownie's suit. "I *should* like something with wings, though."

"Right!" said the gnome. He waved his wand, said a word three times — a very magic one — and touched Anna lightly on the hair, saying, "Change, Miss Waddle-Toes, change! Wear your fancy dress till daybreak!"

Anna felt something funny happening to herself. She was certainly changing. She looked down at herself — and what a dreadful shock she got!

What do you suppose she had changed into? Why, a large yellow duckling with a pair of little flappy wings!

178

"Quack!" cried Anna in dismay. "Quack!"

"Goodness! She's changed into a duck!" shouted the gnome – and a lot more of the little folk came running up. "Look at that!"

"Well, she shouldn't turn her feet in!" said an elf wisely. "She might have known she'd wear a duck's dress for fancy dress, if she waddled about like one! I've often seen her turning in her toes – dreadful! Never mind, Anna! You are small enough to join us and enjoy the party now."

"Quack, quack, quack!" said poor Anna, who felt she would not enjoy the party at all! She could only quack, not talk, and she waddled along turning in her toes all the time, and couldn't dance a bit! She couldn't even fly, for her wings were really much too small. It was all most disappointing!

"How I wish I had never turned my feet in!" she thought to herself, as she tried to dance with a small fairy in butterfly's dress. "Oh dear – my feet are so big that I keep tramping on this dear little fairy's toes!" She tried to say she was sorry, but all she could say was "Quack, quack, quack!"

However, the fairy understood. "Don't mention it," she said politely, and on they danced.

The party would have been simply lovely, but Anna couldn't even eat or drink, because she didn't know how to manage her big beak! It seemed to get in the way so! In fact, it got in her way just as much as her feet did!

"This is a horrible party after all," thought the disappointed little girl. "I can't dance properly – I can't fly – I can't eat this lovely jelly – I can't drink that lovely pink lemonade – and I've never had *pink* lemonade before! I wish I'd never come!"

She sat down on the grass and watched the others dancing. It was a pretty sight – but Anna was sad. She hated being a duckling. It was horrid to waddle about in a clumsy manner when everyone else was dancing so lightly on tiptoe.

"I'll never turn my toes in again, that's certain!" thought Anna. "I didn't know how clumsy it was till I wore this duck fancy dress and was turned into a duck. I won't be so silly again."

When dawn came the fairy folk fled – and Anna was left sitting on the grass alone. She was upset. Suppose she stayed a duckling! Whatever would her mother say?

She waddled back up the garden and into the house. She walked up the stairs. She did not dare to call Mummy, because she knew she would quack. She got into bed, pulled up the clothes with two little arm-wings, and then fell asleep.

And in the morning she was herself again! Yes, really – she had her own feet and arms and everything – she was a little girl and not a duckling. How glad she was!

She jumped out of bed and dressed. Then she ran to tell Mummy her adventure, and dear me – how nicely she turned her toes out as she ran! No more Miss Waddle-Toes for her!

Mummy was sorry she had had such a horrible time at the party. "Never mind," she said, "perhaps next time it will be nicer – especially if you remember not to walk like a duck any more, Anna! Try hard and see if you can walk like a pixie does!"

Anna *is* trying hard – and if you know any little Miss Waddle-Toes just tell them what happened to Anna. They will soon stop turning in their toes, won't they?

Old Mister Glue-Pot

Old Mister Glue-Pot was a gnome who lived in Pillywee Village, on the borders of Fairyland. He kept a paint shop and sold paint in pots, and also very sticky brown glue.

He made this glue himself, and it was so strong that just a touch of it would stick two broken pieces of a jar or dish together in a trice. Mister Glue-Pot had made a lot of money out of this very strong glue.

In fact, he had made such a lot of money that he really didn't bother very much about his shop. He put Snubby the pixie in charge of it, and then he went into his parlour, put his feet up on the mantelpiece, and slept peacefully.

Snubby was not a good shopkeeper. He played about too much. He painted the walls of the shop green and yellow, with blue spots – and will you believe it, Mister Glue-Pot never noticed! Then Snubby discovered the glue. What a game he had with it!

First of all he got some on his hands by mistake – and, dear me, whatever

Snubby touched stuck fast to him. He touched a newspaper and that stuck. He touched two pencils and those stuck! He touched Mister Glue-Pot's best Sunday hat and that stuck. Soon you could hardly see Snubby because so many things were sticking to him!

Snubby managed to unstick himself at last. He stood looking at Mister Glue-Pot's big barrel of glue and grinned. He would have a few jokes with that!

He peeled an orange and then carefully dabbed a spot of glue on each bit of peel. When no one was looking the naughty pixie slipped out of the shop and pressed each bit of peel on the pavement. They all stuck fast. Snubby knew that Mister Plod-Plod, the policeman, would come along that way in a few minutes' time – and old Plod-Plod would certainly try to pick up all those bits of peel!

"It will be fun to see him pulling at them," giggled the naughty pixie to himself. He pressed his snubby nose against the shop window and waited. Soon he heard the plod-plod-plod noise that the policeman's feet made. Up came Mister Plod-Plod and saw the orange peel.

"Now, who's been dropping orange peel about?" he said in his crossest voice. "It is forbidden to do such a thing!"

He looked all round but he could see no one. So Mister Plod-Plod stooped down to pick up all the bits himself – but they were stuck fast to the pavement! Plod-Plod pulled and tugged, and then stared at the peel in amazement. Was it magic? Why wouldn't it come off the pavement?

Plod-Plod took out his knife and cut all the peel away. He put it in his pocket and walked off, looking very puzzled and angry. Snubby laughed till his sides ached.

"That was a good trick!" he said. "Now what else shall I do?"

But before he could do anything else Mister Plod-Plod came back again and asked to see Mister Glue-Pot.

"Mister Glue-Pot," he said sternly, "did you know that someone has been using your glue to stick bits of orange peel to the pavement?"

"Dear me, no!" said Glue-Pot.

"Well, they have," said Plod-Plod. "Please see that you keep an eye on your glue-barrel, Glue-Pot."

"Certainly, certainly," said the old fellow, and he called Snubby to him. "Look after the glue-barrel very, very carefully," he said. Snubby grinned and nodded. He would look after it all right!

Now next door to Mister Glue-Pot's shop was a baker's shop, and outside the door was a very fine mat for people to wipe their feet on. Snubby thought it would be a great joke to dab some glue on it – and then everyone's feet would get stuck there. What fun that would be!

So that night he slipped out with a brush full of glue and daubed the whole mat with it. And you should have seen the muddle there was at the baker's next day!

Dame Trit-Trot and Mister Top-hat went to the baker's shop at the same time, and both trod on the mat together. That was all right – but when they tried to walk off it into the shop they couldn't. The mat went with them! Poor Dame Trit-Trot slipped and slid, trying to get her feet off the sticky mat, and Mister Top-hat suddenly lost his balance and sat down. That was worse than ever! It took the baker two hours to untangle Trit-Trot, Top-hat, and the mat.

How angry they all were! They marched into Mister Glue-Pot's shop and banged on the counter so loudly that Mister Glue-Pot, who was fast asleep in the parlour, woke up, leapt out of his chair, and trod on his poor cat. She scratched him hard and naughty Snubby laughed till he cried.

"If you don't look after your glue better, we shall punish you, Glue-Pot!" cried Trit-Trot, Top-hat, and the baker.

They told him about the sticky mat, and Glue-Pot was full of horror to think that his glue should be used for tricks like that.

"Just see you look after the glue-barrel even better than before," he said to Snubby. And Snubby grinned and said he would. But, the very next day, Snubby slipped across the road to the sweet-shop when it was empty, and dabbed the three chairs with the glue. Oh, what a dreadful thing to do!

That afternoon Snubby watched the people going in to buy sweets. He saw Mrs Lightfoot sit down on a chair. He saw Mister Tap-Tap. He saw the old brownie, Longbeard, sitting down too. They talked together for a little while till their sweets were ready – then they tried to get up to go.

But their chairs stuck to them! They ran out of the shop in horror, taking the chairs with them, though the shopkeeper shouted to them to bring them back. They ran down the street

with the chairs knocking behind them –
and they ran straight into Mister Plod-
Plod, the policeman. And it wasn't long
before he found that it was Mister Glue-
Pot's glue that had done the mischief
again.

He went straight to the paint-shop
and shouted for Mister Glue-Pot.

191

"Pack up your things, take your glue and leave Pillywee Village," he ordered. "We have had enough of these glue tricks, Mister Glue-Pot. Take this cheeky little pixie with you, for I shouldn't be surprised if he had done the mischief."

So poor Mister Glue-Pot and Snubby had to pack up and go. Snubby had to carry the barrel of glue on his back, for Mister Plod-Plod wouldn't let him leave it behind. So over the borders of Fairyland it was carried, and it's still somewhere about today.

Do you know what it is used for? Snubby and Glue-Pot sell it to the chestnut trees in the early spring, so that their buds can be painted with glue to prevent the frost from pinching them. Isn't that a good idea? Snubby paints each bud. You may see him if you look, but if you can't see him, pick a chestnut twig and feel how very strong Mister Glue-Pot's glue is. You *will* be surprised!

Ma Rubbalong deals with Loll-About

"Ma!" called little Rubbalong from where he sat mending boots and shoes. "Here comes Loll-About."

He knew his mother couldn't bear Loll-About. He leaned against everything. He couldn't seem to stand up straight. He was always tired. Ma Rubbalong usually lost her temper when Loll-About came to bring boots to be mended.

"Oho – so it's Loll-About again, is it?" she said, drying her hands quickly. "Well, I said I'd teach him a lesson next time he came along if he hadn't learnt to stand up straight and take his hands out of his pockets."

"He's got some boots with him – he's coming here," said little Rubbalong in delight. "Have you got that lesson ready for him, Ma?"

"I'm getting it ready!" said Ma, briskly, and little Rubbalong saw that she was rubbing the table and the chairs and the doorway and the dresser, in fact every bit of furniture in the room, with a magic duster. What spell had she muttered into it? Rubbalong couldn't imagine!

Loll-About came in at the door. His boots were slung round his neck, and his hands were in his pockets. He slouched as usual.

"Stand up straight and take your hands out of your pockets!" said Ma Rubbalong, sharply. "Have you no manners?"

Loll-About sulkily took his hands out of his pockets. He stood up for a moment, and then he leaned against the table.

It went over with a crash. Loll-About

stared in alarm. Ma Rubbalong gave a snort. "Look at that – did you *have* to loll against the table and knock it over? Stand up straight, I tell you! And pick up all those potatoes that have rolled off on to the floor."

Loll-About set down his boots and picked up the potatoes. He felt rather tired after so much bending, and leaned against the dresser.

Over it went with a tremendous crash! Loll-About almost jumped out of his skin. So did little Rubbalong. Nothing was broken, which seemed rather strange to Rubbalong. Ma spoke angrily to Loll-About.

"*Now* look what you've done! What do you want to go and knock over my dresser for? Lolling about like that!"

"Ma Rubbalong – I'm very sorry," said Loll-About, scared and alarmed at what he had done. "I'm so glad nothing's broken. I'll put the dresser up again for you."

He put it up, with much panting and

puffing. Nobody helped him. Rubbalong went on cobbling shoes and boots and Ma stirred something on the stove.

Loll-About was out of breath when he had heaved the dresser into place. He leaned against Ma's old rocking-chair, panting.

Over went the chair as if it were a skittle – and this time Loll-About went down with it, and bumped himself hard.

"Well!" said Ma Rubbalong, angrily. "What do you suppose you're doing this morning, Loll-About? Do you make a habit of pushing things over?"

"No, Ma, no," said poor Loll-About, getting up in a hurry and putting the chair on its rockers again. "It won't happen again. I won't go near your furniture. I just can't understand it."

He went to stand in the doorway, really afraid of going near a chair or table now. He leaned against it, of course – he just simply couldn't seem to stand up straight by himself.

And will you believe it, the door fell

off its hinges on to the floor! Loll-About stared at it in horror. "Ma Rubbalong! Don't blame me, please don't blame me!" he cried, in alarm. "I only *just* leaned against the doorway – how was I to know the door was so loose?"

"Pick it up, and put it back on its hinges," commanded Ma Rubbalong, and poor Loll-About had to heave the heavy door into place, and spend half an hour putting it right.

"And let me warn you, Loll-About, that if you push my wall down, I'll throw you out of the window," said Ma. "Bless us all – there you go again!"

Poor Loll-About – he had leaned against the broom cupboard, quite tired out with his hard work – and down that went, too, of course! Brooms, brushes, and pans flew out, crashing round him.

Little Rubbalong bent over his cobbling, laughing till the tears ran down his cheeks. Clever old Ma! What shocks she was giving lazy Loll-About! Now he would have to spend twenty minutes standing the cupboard up again and putting everything back.

Ma Rubbalong disappeared into the street outside for a minute while Loll-About was busy with the cupboard. When little Rubbalong saw that she was rubbing the lamp post outside with her magic duster, he almost fell off his stool with laughter.

"You'd better go," said Ma, when Loll-About had put everything back into the cupboard. "If you knock one more thing over I shall most certainly throw you out of the window. I can feel it coming!"

Loll-About went out in alarm. He felt very, very tired now. He came to the lamp post and leaned himself against it for a rest.

CRASH! Down it went, and Loll-About yelled in fright. And, oh my, oh my, there was Mr Plod the policeman coming along, looking very angry indeed.

"What do you want to go about pushing lamp posts down for?" yelled

Mr Plod. "You wait till I catch you!"

But Loll-About didn't wait. He ran off faster than he had run for years. When Mr Plod came up he found little Rubbalong and Ma rolling round the kitchen, almost crying with laughter. He laughed, too, when he heard the joke.

"Well, maybe Loll-About will stop his lazy lolling ways now," said Mr Plod. "I could think of a few other people to use your spell on, Ma, too!"

So could I! I expect you could, as well!

Tiddley-Pom the tailor

O ne day, Very-Small the gnome was walking home along by Bumble-Bee Common, when he came across Bo-Bo the wizard looking very upset.

"What's the matter, Bo-Bo?" asked Very-Small.

"I've lost my spectacles," said Bo-Bo, in a sad voice. "I can't find them anywhere. I can't see at all well without them, too."

"I'll help you to look for them," said Very-Small. "Perhaps you've dropped them in the long grass here."

He looked and looked and looked, but nowhere could he see them. So he went back to Bo-Bo to tell him so. And then he suddenly saw them.

They were pushed high up on Bo-Bo's forehead, and he had forgotten that he had put them there!

Very-Small began to laugh. Then he pointed to the spectacles and said, "Oh, Bo-Bo, your spectacles are up on your forehead. They are not lost at all!"

Bo-Bo was surprised and delighted to find them. He put up his hand, and pulled them down on to his nose. Ah, now he was quite all right again – he could see perfectly well.

"It was very good of you to try to find them for me," he said to the gnome. "I'm sure I would never have guessed they were on my forehead all the time, if you hadn't seen them. I'll give you a little reward."

He felt in his pocket and brought out a little green thing, rather like a marble, but small and soft.

"Here you are," he said to Very-Small. "It's all I have with me. You can have it."

"What is it?" asked Very-Small.

"It's a skippetty-spell," said Bo-Bo. "Be careful how you use it."

Well, Very-Small was always pleased to have any kind of spell, so he took it and said thank you. He ran off whistling, with the spell in his pocket.

Now he hadn't gone very far when he heard a curious noise, and he looked into the ditch to see what made it. Lying on his back there was Tiddley-Pom, the King's tailor, fast asleep. He had taken off his shoes, and they stood beside him.

"My word, Tiddley-Pom will be late at the palace!" said Very-Small to himself. "He's got to measure the King for a new suit at a quarter to three, because he told me so himself this morning. Shall I wake him?"

Very-Small was just going to shake Tiddley-Pom, when he saw the shoes — and a very naughty thought came into his head. He would put the skippetty-spell into them, and see what happened!

So he took it quickly out of his pocket, and broke it in half. He put half in each shoe, and then chuckled loudly. He went to hide behind a tree, and when he was safely there, he threw a fir-cone at Tiddley-Pom, to wake him.

It hit him on the nose, and he awoke with a jump.

"What hit me?" said Tiddley-Pom, sleepily, sitting up and rubbing his eyes. "Was it a drop of rain? What's the time?"

He took out his watch and looked at it. Then he gave a shout of surprise.

"Jumping pigs! It's half-past two! I shall never be at the palace in time!"

Quickly he put on his shoes, and buttoned them tightly. Then he stood up.

Very-Small was watching behind the tree, wondering what was going to happen. He soon saw.

No sooner had Tiddley-Pom put on the shoes than the spell began to work. The tailor hadn't taken six steps before he felt something very funny about his feet. They began to tap the ground and to skip about. Tiddley-Pom didn't know what to make of it all.

Very-Small nearly burst his tight little coat with trying not to laugh out loud. He thought it was very funny to see old Tiddley-Pom dancing away by himself in the road like that, looking most astonished and alarmed.

He followed him without being seen. The poor tailor went hopping and skipping along the road, quite unable to understand why he was doing such funny things. He tried to keep his feet still, but he couldn't. They went on and on skipping and tripping.

"Well, now, what can the matter be with my feet?" said Tiddley-Pom, in a worried voice. "Never before have I known them to behave like this."

He didn't know that it was his shoes which were causing all the trouble. He didn't know what to think about it at all. He was very anxious to get to the palace in time, and so he did his best to keep his feet turned in the right direction. Off they went, prancing and jumping like a pair of ponies. Very-Small thought he had never seen anything so funny in his life.

At last Tiddley-Pom arrived at the palace gates, and danced in past the astonished sentries, who wondered whatever was wrong with the King's tailor. He pranced his way into the throne-room, and tried to keep his feet still whilst he bowed before the King, but he couldn't.

The King stared at him in amazement. He had never seen Tiddley-Pom doing anything so extraordinary before, and he wondered if the tailor had sun-stroke or something.

"What's the matter, Tiddley-Pom?" he asked. "Keep still a moment, please – don't skip all over the place like that, it's most disturbing."

"Oh, please, Your Majesty, I can't help it," said Tiddley-Pom. "My feet just won't stop."

"Nonsense!" said the King. "Stop at once. You're making me feel quite giddy!"

But the tailor couldn't stop, no matter how hard he tried, and soon the tears came into his eyes, and ran down his cheeks. He was very much alarmed, and he was dreadfully afraid that the King would have him sent to prison for disobedience.

Then who should come to pay a call upon the King but Bo-Bo the wizard! He walked into the throne-room, and bowed to His Majesty – and then he turned to stare at Tiddley-Pom's antics.

"Is this a new jester, or a comic dancer you have?" he asked in surprise.

"No," said the King. "It's Tiddley-Pom, my tailor. He says he can't stop his feet from dancing and skipping like that."

The wizard took off his glasses and polished them. Then he put them on again, and looked closely at Tiddley-Pom's feet.

"There's nothing wrong with his feet," he said. "It's his shoes. It looks to me as if there's a skippetty-spell in them. Take off your shoes, Tiddley-Pom."

With the greatest difficulty, the tailor bent down, and took off his shoes, his feet jumping about all the time – but hey presto – as soon as the shoes were off, his feet stopped still, and Tiddley-Pom was himself again. He was so glad that he wept loudly into his handkerchief, whilst the King patted him on the back, and told him not to mind.

"This is a funny thing," said Bo-Bo, peering into the shoes, and taking out two bits of green. "This is the same spell that I gave to Very-Small not an hour ago. He must have put it into Tiddley-Pom's shoes. How very naughty of him!"

"Fetch him here," said the King, frowning.

Two servants went to find Very-Small, and there he was at the gate of the palace, waiting to see the tailor come skipping out again. He was very much surprised to be led before the King, for he hadn't dreamed that his naughty trick would be found out.

"I am ashamed of you, Very-Small," said the King. "You ought to know better than this. You have made Tiddley-Pom very unhappy and worried, to say nothing of making him late in measuring me for my new suit."

"But he looked so funny," said Very-Small, beginning to giggle.

"Perhaps you'd like to try the shoes yourself, then," said Bo-Bo, slipping the spell into them again, and holding them out to Very-Small. "I'm sure you'll find them funnier still when you've got them on. Give Tiddley-Pom your own shoes, and take his."

Very-Small looked alarmed, but he had to obey. Tiddley-Pom put on the gnome's shoes, and Very-Small put on the skippetty-shoes. Soon he was skipping and dancing all over the room!

How everyone laughed! How the King roared, and Bo-Bo chuckled! As for Tiddley-Pom, he laughed so much that he burst a button off his coat.

Only Very-Small didn't laugh – he found that it wasn't funny at all. But he had to wear the skippetty-shoes for the rest of the day, and when at last he was allowed to take them off, he was so tired and so sorry for himself, that I think it will be a very long time before he tries any more tricks of that sort again!

As for the spell, he threw it into the dustbin, and nobody has ever seen it since.

The funny balloon-face

Katie came in from her school party, calling for her mother. "Mummy! Look what I've got! A bag of sweets, a banana, and a tiny doll. And oh – do look at my balloon. It's got such a funny face!"

So it had. It was a big, grinning face painted on one side of the balloon. It bobbed about on the string as Katie pulled it here and there.

She had to go to bed then, because it was really very late. She put the balloon with her dolls and her toys and then shut the door.

The toys looked at the balloon-face in alarm. "What is it?" whispered the clockwork mouse. "I don't like it."

"I'm Bobabout the balloon-face," said the balloon in a squeaky sort of voice. Then he bobbed about over the mouse, bouncing all the way along his back.

"Don't!" said the mouse. "You're horrid. I don't like you. I don't like your big, grinning face either."

"I shall hide in corners at night and bob out at you," said Bobabout. "I shall look in at the windows of the dolls' house and scare the dolls there. I shall . . ."

"You'll do nothing of the sort," said the clockwork clown. "You'll just behave yourself if you come to live with us! Now – sit down in that corner and stop grinning. It isn't funny, and we shan't like you if you talk like that!"

But do you suppose the big balloon would do as he was told? Not he! He went and squashed his face against the dolls' house windows and all the tiny dolls squealed in fright and ran to hide under the beds. He chased the clockwork mouse, bouncing all over the floor after him, pulling dreadful faces as he went. He was really most unpleasant.

The sailor doll went and whispered to the pink rabbit. The pink rabbit looked very startled.

"*What* did you say?" he asked. "Something about sticking a pin into Balloon-Face? Why? What would happen if we did?"

"He'd go POP!" said the clockwork clown. "He'd go pop and disappear. All that would be left of him would be a tiny bit of rubber. Let's prick him with a pin. He's perfectly horrid. I'd like him to go pop."

"Yes – but what would Katie say?" said the rabbit. "I'm very fond of Katie. She might be upset if we pricked her balloon and made him go pop and disappear."

"I hadn't thought of that," said the clockwork clown. "Yes, she might be sad. I like her, too. Oh dear – we'd better not prick old Balloon-Face with a pin then. But it would be such a good punishment for him. Look at him bobbing after the toy cat now. She's really scared. He does make such horrid faces!"

The pink rabbit and the sailor doll went over to the balloon and punched him hard. But he only grinned more than ever and bounced so high in the air that he hit the ceiling.

He was most annoying all that night and the next day, too, while Katie was at school. And then the pink rabbit noticed something. He spoke to the clown about it.

"Clown – don't you think that Balloon-Face has gone smaller? He doesn't seem quite as huge as he was – his grin is smaller, too."

"Dear me, yes," said the clown. "How very odd! I do hope he goes smaller still!"

Well, as you may have guessed, there was just a very tiny leak in the balloon and the air was gradually going out of him, so that he wasn't as much blown up as he had been. It was really rather strange to see him slowly going a bit smaller and a bit smaller.

By that night he was half the size. He was very worried. He couldn't bounce about quite so much now, and although he tried once or twice to chase the clockwork mouse, he couldn't catch him. The toys went and looked at him.

"He's not nearly so big," said the teddy bear, pleased. "He'll soon be down to nothing!"

"It serves him right," said the pink rabbit. "He thought himself so big that he could behave as he liked. But now he can't."

"I've a little tiny leak somewhere," said Bobabout, the balloon, in rather a small voice. "Could you blow me up again, please? It's such a tiny leak that it won't matter at all, so long as I'm blown up when I go down."

"What! Blow up a silly, unkind thing like you and let you go bouncing about all over us again, staring in at the dolls' house windows, and chasing the clockwork mouse?" cried the clown. "Of course we shan't. We *might* have done so if you'd been nice and kind."

The balloon went so small that he couldn't even move. He was just a little heap of rubber on the end of a string. The toys couldn't even see his grinning face. That had got smaller and smaller, too, and the big smile had gone, till now there was almost no face at all.

"I feel rather sorry for him," said the mouse, who was a kindhearted little thing. "I suppose we couldn't blow him up just a tiny bit? He's lost his voice now. It must be very horrid for him."

"Well — we'll blow him up just a teeny-tiny bit," said the bear. "I'll try first because I'm fat and I've got a lot of breath."

So he blew where the string was tied to the balloon. He had quite a lot of breath, and old Balloon-Face swelled up at once. Not very much — but enough to make his face come back. The toys looked at him closely.

"He hasn't got that horrid grin any more," said the bear, "he's got quite a nice smile. Balloon-Face, how do you feel?"

"I feel sorry I behaved as I did," said Bobabout, in a very small voice. "I don't feel like grinning and bouncing any more. Blow me up a bit more, please, Teddy."

The bear blew again and then the pink rabbit took a turn. Balloon-Face got quite big. His smile grew broader – but it was still a nice smile.

"That's enough blow," said the bear. "Don't make him any bigger, or he might be silly again. How do you feel now, Balloon-Face?"

"*Much* better," said the balloon, beginning to bob about merrily again. The clockwork mouse ran into a corner at once. "Don't blow him up any more, please don't!" he squeaked.

"We won't," said the bear. "And just

you listen to me, Balloon-Face – that little leak you've got will make you go down small again, and we shan't blow you up next time if you don't behave as a nice balloon should! So just be careful how you grin and bob and bounce."

Bobabout knew he had got to be good and sensible. Now the toys blow him up every time he goes down flat – and dear me, how surprised Katie is, having a balloon that lasts such a very long time!

The surprising saucepan

Once, when Nippy the goblin tiptoed by Dame Dozy's window, he saw her magic saucepan sitting on the kitchen stove.

Now this was a marvellous saucepan, because you had only to drop a bit of potato peel into it, and a tealeaf or two, and then say what you wanted for dinner, and the saucepan would at once cook you a stew, or a boiled apple dumpling, or anything else you asked for!

Nippy stopped when he saw that saucepan. He had nothing in his larder that night for his supper, nothing at all. He was very hungry. Suppose he borrowed that saucepan for an hour or two? Dame Dozy would never know!

He popped his head in at the window. Nobody there. He went to the back door. There was a sheet of paper pinned to it. Nippy read what it said. "Back at seven o'clock, signed DD. Ooooh, that's three hours ahead! Time for me to borrow the saucepan, get it to cook me a tasty stew, and a pudding afterwards, and take it back without anyone knowing. What a chance!"

He hopped in at the window and took the saucepan off the stove. It wasn't a very big one. Nippy wondered if he ought to wrap it up in paper so that no one would see him carrying a saucepan. They might wonder where he had got it.

Then a good idea came to him. "I'll wear it as a hat!" he thought. "It's a red saucepan, and really will look quite like a hat. Yes – it fits me well!"

So, wearing the saucepan, he hopped out of the window again and went across the common to his home.

But the saucepan began to feel a bit

heavy. It had felt so light at first. Now it quite weighed down his head.

Nippy moved it a little, and it fell right over his nose! "Bother you, Saucepan!" he said, and tried to get it off.

But it seemed to get heavier and heavier, and poor Nippy couldn't lift it off his head. He stopped still and tried his hardest.

"It *is* getting heavier – and it's getting bigger, too!" he said, in a fright. "Oh my, oh my, it's over my shoulders now. I must get it off, I must, I must!"

But by now it was so terribly heavy that he couldn't even stand up. He had to sit down. The saucepan had grown so big that it was now down to his waist!

Poor Nippy. He bowed down lower and lower under the heavy weight, and soon the saucepan reached the ground. Nippy couldn't be seen at all! He was completely hidden under the saucepan!

He began to cry. "What shall I do? I can't get out! It's dark under here and I'm frightened. Oh, get away, you horrid saucepan, how dare you behave like this!"

The saucepan stopped growing. It settled down over Nippy, and stayed quite still and quiet. Nippy hit it with his fists, but it took no notice at all. It just sat there and waited patiently.

"Perhaps it will grow small and light again after a while," thought Nippy hopefully.

But it didn't. So Nippy had to stay there, underneath. There was nothing else he could do.

Now when Dame Dozy came home she missed her saucepan at once.

She told Mother Daws who was with her. "My saucepan's gone! Never mind, there's some bread and cheese in the larder. We'll have that for our supper."

"But, Dame Dozy, don't you want to go and find your magic saucepan?" cried Mother Daws. "Why, it's very, very valuable. You must really find the thief."

"No hurry," said Dame Dozy, getting

the bread and cheese. "My saucepan can look after itself. It's got a good way with thieves. I never worry about that saucepan of mine!"

She didn't. She and Mother Daws had a good meal, then Mother Daws went home. Dame Dozy went to bed and slept well.

But poor Nippy didn't sleep at all! The ground was damp and cold. He couldn't see a single star because of the big saucepan over him. He was very hungry and thirsty. How he hated that saucepan!

Now, in the morning, some pixies and elves came walking over the common. They were surprised to see an enormous red saucepan upside down on the common.

"Look at that!" they cried. "What's it doing here? Let's move it."

But they couldn't. It was far too heavy.

"Oh, do move it and let me out!" begged Nippy. "Quick, let me out!"

The little folk were surprised to hear Nippy's voice. They stood looking at the saucepan.

"It's Dame Dozy's saucepan!" suddenly cried a pixie. "But it's gone big! We'd better tell her!"

"No, don't, don't!" wailed Nippy, scared.

But the elves and pixies had run off to Dame Dozy's cottage. She wasn't at all surprised to see them or to hear what they had to say.

"I was expecting someone to come along and tell me where my saucepan was," she said. "It has a very good way of its own with little robbers! I'll come and get it."

So she went to the common. She tapped on the saucepan.

"Who's below?'" she asked in a stern voice.

"N-n-n-n-n-nippy!" answered Nippy, in a small voice. "I j-j-j-just b-b-borrowed your s-s-saucepan for a bit, Dame Dozy, and it did this to me."

"A very good thing to do," said Dame Dozy. "I hope it will be a lesson to you, Nippy, to keep your hands off things that don't belong to you unless you get permission first. I've a good mind to leave you here all day!"

But she didn't. She made her red saucepan go small again and set poor Nippy free.

"You be careful of saucepans in future!" she said.

And poor Nippy is so scared of them he won't even use his own at home. He boils his potatoes in his kettle!

Goldie and the water sprite

Goldie was a fine goldfish. He lived in a big glass globe on the playroom bookcase, and swam about by himself all day long. In the globe was some green water-weed, three water-snails, an empty sea shell, and at the bottom, a few clean, white stones.

Goldie was proud of his home. Everyone who came to the playroom said how pretty it looked, with all the green water-weed floating about the water. The goldfish belonged to Minnie and Beth, the two little girls who lived in the house.

At night he had a lovely time. All the toys used to creep from their shelves and out of the toy cupboard and play games with each other. Goldie used to watch them, and often the dolls would climb up to his shelf and talk to him.

Sometimes they would bring with them a little floating duck, and float it on Goldie's water. The duck loved that, and Goldie was pleased when the little creature dived down into the water and said what a beautiful fish he was.

One day Minnie and Beth, who were twins, had a birthday. Their Auntie Susan gave them a lovely toy. It was a circus, with elephants, horses, clowns, lions and bears. There was a band too, made of little men, each with a trumpet, drum or horn. Minnie and Beth thought the circus was lovely, and they played with it all day long.

When bedtime came they left it out on the floor. As soon as the house was quiet and dark the toys ran up to see what the circus was like. Then all the elephants, horses and clowns came to life!

"We'll give you a fine show!" said one of the clowns to the toys around. "Come along and sit down. Now, band, strike up and play a merry tune!"

The band struck up and soon a lively march was heard in the playroom. The circus began. The elephants performed, the horses danced, the lions and bears did their tricks and the clowns made everyone laugh.

Goldie saw that something was happening, and he pushed his nose against the side of the glass globe and tried to see what it was. He heard the sound of the band and it made him excited.

"Oh, I *wish* I could see what they're doing!" he thought, waving his tail from side to side. "Why doesn't someone come up and tell me? What lovely music! I feel as if I want to go mad with joy when I hear it!"

The band made him feel so frisky that he began to rush all about the water. Then suddenly he gave a great leap upwards, and jumped right out of the glass globe!

Flop! He fell on the floor and all the breath was shaken out of his glittering body. "Ah!" he thought. "Now I shall be able to go and see what all the excitement is about!"

But, alas for Goldie! He found that he couldn't breathe out of the water! He began to gasp, and wriggled about on the floor, wondering why he couldn't swim.

The toys heard the flop and looked round. The circus stopped in a hurry.

"Ooh, it's Goldie!" cried the teddy bear in a fright. "He's jumped out and he can't get back!"

"Whatever shall we do?" said a clown, hurrying up to the struggling fish. "We can't get him back to the water, he's too big and slippery."

"Oh, Goldie, dear Goldie, you'll die out of the water," sobbed one of the dolls.

All the toys stood round the gasping goldfish, wondering what to do. Then the little floating duck had an idea.

"Let's fetch the water sprite who lives

all alone out in the pond," it said. "Perhaps she will know what to do."

So a wooden soldier was sent to fetch the sprite, and she soon came hurrying in, her wet hair hanging down her back. When she saw the poor goldfish on the floor, she was very upset.

"We must get him quickly back to the water," she said, "or else he will die. Where does he live?"

"In the glass globe on the bookcase," said the teddy bear, pointing upwards.

"Goodness!" said the sprite. "We can't get him up there! What in the world shall we do?"

She looked round the playroom, and saw the dolls' house. She ran inside, and in a trice was out again.

"There's a bath in there," she said to the teddy bear. "Fetch it out quickly. Then take some jugs from the dresser in the doll's house kitchen, and fill them with water from the glass globe. Put the water in the bath and fill it as quickly as you can. Then we'll lift the goldfish

into it. He's nearly as big as the bath is, but if he lies still, he will be all right till morning."

All the toys ran to do what she said. The dolls' tin bath was dragged out, and the little jugs were taken from the dresser. Soon they were filled with water, which was poured into the bath.

All this time Goldie lay on the floor. He was so weak and breathless now that he could hardly move. He felt sure he was going to die.

At last the bath was full.

"Now!" cried the sprite. "The teddy, the clown and one of the dolls must lift Goldie up gently and carry him to the bath. Put him into the water, and see if he is all right."

"Oh, poor Goldie, he's dead, I'm sure he's dead!" wept the fairy doll, as she saw the goldfish lying quite still. The teddy bear, the big doll and a clown went to him and lifted him gently in their arms. They carried him to the bath very slowly, for he was heavy.

Then they slipped him into the water.

All the toys crowded round to see if he would come to life. For some time he made no movement at all. Then, very feebly, he moved his tail and opened his mouth to take in water.

"He's alive, he's alive!" cried the toys in delight. "We've saved him!"

In half an hour's time Goldie was quite all right again, and wasn't he astonished to find himself in the dolls' bath! The teddy bear explained to him what had happened, and he was very grateful.

"I'll lie here quite still till the morning," he said. "Then I expect Minnie and Beth will find me, and put me back into my glass globe again. It's really very kind of you all to have saved me."

"It was the water sprite that really saved your life," said the teddy. "It was her idea to put you into the bath. We should never have thought of it."

Next morning Minnie and Beth found

Goldie lying in their dolls' bath. They *were* astonished!

"Oh, look, Mummy!" they cried. "Goldie's got out of his globe to have a bath! Isn't he funny! Let's put him back again. However did he get there?"

But Mummy couldn't answer *that* question. She was just as puzzled as the twins.

That isn't quite all the story. When the water sprite came to ask about Goldie the next day, she slid down into the fish's globe and swam up to him.

"Ooh!" she said, with delight. "Your water feels so nice and warm after the cold pond outside, Goldie! It's so lonely there too – there isn't a single fish I can talk to."

"Well," said Goldie, "I'm rather lonely here myself – wouldn't you like to come and share my home with me? You could live in that empty sea shell at the bottom."

"Oh, I'd *love* to!" cried the sprite, and

she straightaway crept into the shell and cuddled there. And now Goldie and the sprite live together as happy as can be. If you want to see her in the daytime, you'll know where to look – in the sea shell that lies at the bottom of Goldie's globe!

Oh, what a pity!

Tessie had a bicycle, and all the other boys and girls thought she was very lucky, because it really was a nice one.

At first she lent it to anyone who wanted to try and ride it, but when Harry had dented the mudguard, and Jane had broken a pedal, Tessie's mother said she was not to lend it to any child except in her own garden.

Susan was cross when she heard this. "Oh, how mean of your mother!" she said. "She might let you lend it in the road, Tessie!"

"Mummy isn't mean," said Tessie, who would never let anyone say a word against her mother. "It's just that she paid a lot of money for my bike, and she doesn't want it spoilt. She's not mean."

"Well, you ask me to tea and then I can ride your bike in the garden," said Susan. So Tessie told her mother that Susan wanted to come to tea so that she could ride the bicycle.

"Susan always wants to push in and get her own way," said Tessie's mother. "No, I can't have her to tea just yet, Tessie. You are having your cousin for the day this week, and Harry is coming to tea on Tuesday. You can't have Susan."

Susan was cross. "Well, I said it before and I say it again – your mother is mean!" she said to Tessie. Tessie walked off without a word. She was not going to quarrel with Susan, but she wasn't going to stay with her if she said things like that.

Susan soon tried to make Tessie friends with her again, because she so badly wanted to ride Tessie's bicycle. So she gave her a sweet, and told her that she was the nicest girl in the class.

When Tessie was sucking the sweet and was nice and friendly once more, Susan asked for a ride.

"Let me have a little ride, just a tiny little ride on your bike," she said. "We'll wait till all the other boys and girls have gone, Tessie, then no one will see. I'll ride it down the lane, that's all. Please do let me."

"Mummy said I wasn't to," said Tessie.

"Well," said Susan, thinking of another idea. "Well, Tessie, you just turn your back for a minute – and I'll hop on the bike and ride off without you seeing. Then it won't matter, because, you see, you won't have *lent* me the bike, I shall have taken it. Please, please, do let me have a ride, Tessie. You're so lucky to have a bike."

"Well," said Tessie, hardly liking to say no, because she saw how much Susan wanted a ride. "Well – just this once, then."

She turned her back. Susan jumped

241

on to the bike and rode away down the lane. How fast she rode! How grand she felt!

Just as she passed a field-gate a cow came out, the first of a herd driven out by the farmer. Susan was so frightened that she wobbled, and fell off. Crash! She fell on her side and grazed her arm badly, and tore her dress.

Tessie heard the crash and turned. She ran to Susan and helped her up. "Oh – I knew I shouldn't have let you ride my bike," she said. "I knew I shouldn't! Look at your poor arm – and what will your mother say to your torn dress?"

The bicycle was not hurt, which was lucky. Susan picked it up, brushed her frock down, and looked at her bleeding arm. "Bother!" she said. "That tiresome cow! It made me fall off."

"Well, you shouldn't have been on the bike, should you, really?" said Tessie, taking it. "You shouldn't have told me to turn my head away so that you could take it without my seeing you. It's a good thing the bike isn't damaged. Mummy *would* have been cross with you – and with me, too, for disobeying her."

Susan went home, trying to hide her torn dress and grazed arm. But her mother saw them both at once.

"Susan! What have you done to your arm? Did you fall down? And how did you tear your dress?"

"I was riding Tessie's bike," said Susan, not liking to tell her mother a story. "A cow came out of a gate and scared me, and I fell off."

"Susan, you are *not* to ride other people's bicycles," said her mother, at once. "For two reasons – one is that you may damage someone else's bike, and the other is that you haven't had enough practice in riding, and until you have you are not to ride in the road. You might have a bad accident."

"I shouldn't," said Susan, looking sulky.

"Now, do you understand, Susan?" said her mother. "I mean it. You are *not* to ride Tessie's bicycle, or anyone else's. One day you shall have one of your own, and then you can practise riding it round and round your own garden till you can ride well enough to go out into the road. Be patient and wait till then."

Susan didn't feel at all patient. How could she wait perhaps for years for a bicycle? She knew that a bicycle was expensive, and she knew that her mother hadn't a lot of money to spare. She might have to wait till she was twelve before she had a bicycle — and she wasn't even nine till next week! How she wished she could have a bicycle for her ninth birthday! That would be grand.

Her arm soon healed. Her dress was mended. Once or twice her mother warned her to remember what she had said about Tessie's bicycle.

"You will remember that I don't want you to ride Tessie's bicycle again, won't you?" she said. "And I hear that Tessie's mother has asked her not to lend it to anyone, too – so on no account must you borrow it, Susan."

Susan didn't say anything. She meant to have another ride whenever she could! Her mother noticed that she said nothing and spoke sharply.

"Susan! Will you promise me not to ride on Tessie's bicycle?" she said.

"All right," said Susan, sulkily. How tiresome to have to promise! "I wish I could have a bike for my birthday next week, Mummy! Tessie was only nine when she had hers."

"Bicycles are so expensive," said Susan's mother. "And you are not very old yet. There is plenty of time for you to have a bicycle, Susan!"

Susan didn't ask Tessie for a ride any more that week. She watched her riding to and from school very enviously, but she didn't beg for a turn, too. She didn't want to upset Tessie, or to break her own promise.

The next week came. The day before her birthday came, Susan told everyone it was her birthday the next day, and she felt excited because she knew her mother was making her a cake with nine candles on it, and she thought she was having a work-basket and a new book, too.

Now, as Susan went home from school that afternoon, she suddenly saw Tessie's bicycle leaning against the wall that ran round Harry's garden in the main road! Yes, there it was, bright and shining. Tessie must have gone in to see Harry's white mice.

"The road's empty. I'll just jump on Tessie's bike and have a little ride!" thought Susan. "No one will know. I'll go round the corner and back."

Quite forgetting her promise, Susan jumped on the bicycle and rode down the road. She went fast, pedalling up and down strongly. She rang her bell at the corner. Ting-a-ling-a-ling! It sounded fine.

Then she put the brakes on to see if they worked. But they didn't work very well. Tessie had been told that she must take her bicycle to the shop to have the brakes put right, or else she might have an accident.

"Now I'd better go back," thought Susan to herself, and turned to go back. She had pedalled up the hill, and now it would be fun to go down it without pedalling at all!

She simply *flew* down! It was quite a steep hill. Suddenly, round the corner, came the big old cart-horse belonging to the farmer, dragging a heavy cart behind him.

Susan wobbled. She rang her bell but the horse took no notice. She put on the brakes to slow the bicycle down – but they didn't work! The bicycle flew on and on, and it seemed as if the big horse and cart blocked up the whole of the road.

Just as she reached the horse, Susan tried to jump off the bike. But it was going too fast for her to jump properly. She slipped, the bicycle flew straight into the alarmed horse, and Susan herself rolled over and over and over towards the side of the road.

She sat up, gasping, looking at herself to see if she was hurt. But she wasn't! There didn't seem even to be a bruise or a scratch.

Then she looked round for the bicycle. But oh, what a pity, it was completely spoilt! The frightened horse had reared up when Susan had run into it, and had brought its heavy, enormous hoofs down on to the bicycle. The wheels were buckled and broken. The handle was twisted. The right pedal was off and the left one was bent.

"Oh! Look at Tessie's bike!" said Susan, with tears in her eyes. The farmer was trying to pull it from his horse's feet. He thought the bicycle was Susan's.

"I'm afraid your bike's done for," he said. "Why did you ride so fast down

the hill? That was silly of you. You frightened my horse terribly. He might have run away."

Susan didn't know what to do. Crying bitterly, she dragged the poor, broken bike home at last, and her mother came running out to see whatever was the matter.

"Oh, Mummy – oh, Mummy – look at Tessie's bike!" wept Susan. "I broke my promise. I took it when Tessie was at Harry's – and I ran into a horse, and the horse stamped on the bike. Oh, Mummy, what shall I do?"

Her mother looked in horror at the bicycle. "Are you hurt?" she said to Susan. Susan shook her head. "Well, you might easily have been killed, Susan. And *look* at Tessie's bike! Whatever will her father and mother say?"

"I don't know, I don't know!" wailed Susan. "Oh, why did I disobey you and break my promise? Tell me what I'm to do!"

Susan's mother looked very grave. She set the broken bicycle by the fence, and took Susan's arm. "Come with me," she said. "I will show you what you must do."

She took Susan to a shed, which was locked. She unlocked it. Inside was a brand-new, very beautiful, shining bicycle! Susan gave a gasp when she saw it.

"Look," said her mother. "Daddy and I bought this for your birthday tomorrow, for a big surprise. Now, Susan, I am afraid you must take it to Tessie instead, because you have completely spoilt *her* bicycle. Maybe we can get Tessie's mended up for you – I don't know – but you will certainly have to give up your new bicycle to Tessie."

Oh, what a pity! Oh, what a terrible pity to have to give up such a beautiful bicycle to somebody else, all because of a moment's disobedience and a broken promise. How Susan cried! How she wept and wailed! But she knew her mother was right. It was the only thing to do.

So now Tessie has Susan's beautiful bicycle, and Susan is waiting to hear if Tessie's old one can be mended. Poor Susan – it was very hard for her, wasn't it, but, as her mother said, you never know *what* may happen if you are disobedient, or break a solemn promise!

It's a rainy day

"**I**'m sure Aunt Twinkle will make us go and do all the shopping for her today," said Snip. "She said if it was fine we'd have to go."

"And it's as fine as can be," said Snap, looking out of the window.

"And we did want to finish making that aeroplane!" said Snorum. "Shopping is a perfect nuisance. I don't want to go. Why doesn't it rain?"

"I say, you've given me an idea!" said Snip at once. "Half a minute. I'll be back!"

He ran downstairs and out into the garden shed. When he came back he was carrying two watering cans. Snap and Snorum stared in surprise.

"Now, listen," said Snip. "The kitchen window is just below our playroom, and Aunt Twinkle will be working there all morning. Now, suppose we fill a watering can, and tip it out of our playroom window, what will Aunt Twinkle see down in the kitchen below if she looks out of *her* window?"

"Rain!" said Snap and Snorum at once, and they roared with laughter. "The water will sprinkle down out of the can, and she'll think it's raining. Hurray!"

"Yes," said Snip, pleased. "We can take it in turns to fill the first can and empty it, and while it's making rain for Aunt Twinkle to see, we'll be filling the second can, so that the rain never stops! One of us must go down and tell Aunt Twinkle it's raining so that we can't go shopping!"

Well, what a trick to think of! Just like those three mischievous imps!

Snip began to fill a can. Snap stood ready to take it to the window. Snorum ran down to the kitchen to his aunt.

"Ah, there you are, Snorum," said Aunt Twinkle. "I want you to go shopping for me, all three of you. There's a long list this morning."

"You said we needn't go if it was raining," said Snorum.

"Well, it isn't," said his aunt.

And just at that very minute Snap took the watering can to the window upstairs, tipped it up, and down came a great spatter of drops, looking for all the world like rain!

"There – look – it's started to *pour*," said Snorum, trying not to giggle.

Aunt Twinkle looked up in astonishment. "Well, I *am* surprised. It didn't look a bit like rain. Perhaps it will stop in a minute."

But it didn't, of course, because upstairs Snip and Snap were hard at work filling the cans and emptying them out of the window. Soon the kitchen window below was running with drops, and Aunt Twinkle thought

it must be really pouring!

"It looks as if it's set in for the morning," she said. "Very well, you needn't go shopping for me. I don't want you to get wet through. Go back upstairs and play with the others."

Snorum was glad. Up he went, and told them the good news. "We'll just empty a can out occasionally now," he said. "Just to keep the drops running down the kitchen window. Come on – let's get on with the aeroplane."

Now, after about half an hour, someone came up the garden path. It was Mister Kindly, and Aunt Twinkle was very pleased to see him.

"I've just come to ask if you'll let Snip, Snap and Snorum come with me and have dinner in the town, and go to see a conjuring show afterwards," said Mister Kindly. "I've got the tickets."

"But it's pouring with rain!" said Aunt Twinkle, looking at the drops running down the kitchen window.

"Oh, no, it's not," said Mister Kindly,

in surprise. "Look – I'm not a bit wet.
It's fine and dry. I can't *think* why
your window is so wet. A pipe must be
leaking just above it."

He went out to see and, of course,
he saw the spout of the watering can
sticking out of the playroom window
above, and he guessed at once what
the three imps were up to. They didn't
want to go shopping!

"I suppose they don't like going
shopping in the rain?" said Mister
Kindly, coming back.

"No. They haven't got macs, so they
get wet through," said Aunt Twinkle.
"But I can't understand why you are so
dry, Mister Kindly. It really *is* pouring
down with rain!"

"It isn't," said Mister Kindly, and he
told her what he had seen. "You've
got three selfish, lazy little imps here,
Mrs Twinkle. *I'm* not going to take
them to dinner and to a conjuring
show! I'll ask Pippin, Poppin and Skip
next door instead."

And with that out went Mister Kindly.

Aunt Twinkle called Snip, Snap and Snorum down to her. "Mister Kindly just called in," she said. "He had tickets for a conjuring show this afternoon, and wanted to take you all to it, and out to dinner first. But I told him how you hated to go out in the rain – so he's gone next door to ask Pippin, Poppin and Skip. They'll *love* it!"

"Oh, don't let *them* go!" cried Snip. "We'd love to go! Rain won't hurt us."

"Oh, yes it will," said Aunt Twinkle, firmly. "If you can't go out into the rain to do my shopping – you can't possibly walk all the way to the next village. You'd be *soaked*!"

Snip, Snap and Snorum went back upstairs looking very gloomy indeed.

Aunt Twinkle called after them. "And would you like to take those watering cans back to the shed? You won't need them any more now."

What a shock they got! They did feel

ashamed.

"We'd better go and say we're sorry," said Snip, when they had taken back the watering cans. "We shan't get any cakes for tea if we don't!"

So they walked into the kitchen again.

"We're sorry, Aunt Twinkle," said Snip. "Very sorry. And we'll go and do your shopping this afternoon, we promise we will!"

Would you believe it, just before they set out, it began to *pour* with rain! It simply fell down in sheets. Real rain this time, not watering can rain!

But Aunt Twinkle made them go shopping just the same. "Promises must be kept, rain or no rain," she said. "It serves you right for being mean. Off you go, all of you, with my big umbrella between you."

And there they go, very sorry for themselves indeed. Watering can rain indeed! What a thing to do!

The little roundy man

Billy, Joan and Tom were out for a picnic in the woods one day when their big adventure happened. They didn't know it was going to happen at all, and it all began when Joan wanted to play hide-and-seek.

"All right," said Billy. "I'll hide my eyes first. Call 'Cuckoo' when you are ready."

He hid his eyes, and waited for the others to shout, "Cuckoo." Tom ran behind a big bramble bush, and crouched down. Joan found a hollow tree with a hole just big enough to squeeze through. She got in, and called, "Cuckoo! Cuckoo!"

Billy opened his eyes and began to

look for the others. He soon found Tom, but didn't catch him, for Tom got home first. Then he looked for Joan.

Now as soon as Joan got into the hollow tree she looked about her, but at first it was too dark to see anything. Then she saw a very strange thing. There was a little shelf in the tree, just about the level of her head – and on it was a pair of little blue shoes!

Joan thought that was very strange indeed. Who would hide shoes in a hollow tree? And who had built the neat little shelf? It was very odd. Perhaps the fairies lived nearby and the shoes belonged to them.

Joan began to feel excited. She forgot about the game of hide-and-seek and called to Billy.

"I say, Billy!" she cried. "There's something funny in this tree. Come and see."

Billy and Tom went racing over to look. When they saw the little shelf and the shoes on it they were full of surprise. Billy took the shoes from the shelf, and helped Joan out of the tree. Then all three looked at the shoes.

They were very beautiful, made of the softest leather, and were the brightest blue you can imagine. They had silver buckles on, and when Billy turned the shoes upside down, he saw that they had never been worn.

"Do you know, Joan, I believe they would just fit you!" said Tom. "Do try them on."

So Joan took off her own shoes, and slipped on the blue ones. They fitted her perfectly. She stood up and began to dance about in them – then a funny thing happened.

The shoes suddenly began to walk away with her. She felt her feet being taken down the path that led to the heart of the woods. She tried to turn back to the boys, but the shoes kept her feet going to the middle of the wood.

"Joan! Come back!" called the boys. "Don't go that way! You'll get lost!"

"Help me, help me!" cried Joan in a fright. "I can't come back! The shoes won't let me! Billy! Tom! Come and hold me so that I can't go any further!"

The boys raced after Joan — but as soon as they were almost up to her the shoes on her feet began to hurry, and somehow or other Joan found herself running faster than she had ever run in her life before.

"Quick! Quick!" she shouted to the panting boys, "I'm being taken away. These shoes are magic! Oh, catch me, Billy, and take these shoes off!"

But the boys couldn't catch Joan, no matter how they hurried. In a few moments she was quite out of sight in the dark wood, and soon they could no longer hear her cries for help. They stopped and looked at one another.

"Oh my goodness," said Billy. "This is a dreadful thing! Where has poor Joan gone to? And oh, Tom — we're quite lost! I don't know where we are, do you?"

"No," said Tom, looking all round. "And isn't it dark, Billy? The trees are so thick that not a ray of sun gets through. Oh dear, what *are* we going to do about poor little Joan? It's no good going after her – and if we try to get help we shall only get more lost."

"Well, we must do *something*," said Billy. "Look, there's a kind of path over there. Let's follow that and see if it brings us anywhere."

The two boys went down the narrow, winding path. After a few minutes they came to a curious house. It was perfectly round, and had one chimney at the top. There was a window and a door, and that was all. It was about twice as high as they were, and the boys thought it was the funniest place they had ever seen.

"What shall we do?" asked Billy. "Shall we knock?"

"Yes," said Tom, and he walked boldly up to the door. He knocked loudly, like a postman – rat-a-tat-tat, rat-a-tat-tat.

At once the door flew open and the strangest little creature looked out. He was almost as round as his house, and he wore big round spectacles on his funny little nose.

"Now, now!" he said, crossly. "I thought you were the postman. What do you want?"

"Well, it's rather a long story," said Billy. "But we would be so glad if you would help us."

And he told the little round man all about the shoes that had run away with Joan.

"Dear, dear, dear!" said the little man, and he took his glasses off and polished them. "You'd better come in and sit down. I may be able to help you a little. This is a very serious matter."

The two boys went into the round house. It was the funniest place inside, quite round, with no corners at all. There was one room downstairs and one room upstairs. Everything was round. The table was round, the stools were round, the carpet was round and the clock was round. There was a cat by the fire and it was almost round too, it was so fat and sleek.

"Now I had better tell you at once that I am afraid those blue shoes belong to Candle-Shoe the old magician. He plays a trick with them whenever he wants someone to help him with his spells. He puts them in a hollow tree or under a bush, and whoever finds them and tries them on is immediately led to him in his underground cave. Of course, he wants one of the fairy folk, not a little girl – but if he thinks she will do for him, he will keep her for years to help him with his spells."

"Oh my!" said Billy in a fright. "But whatever shall we do, little man?"

"My name is Roundy," said the little man. "Well, I must see what I can do to help you. I will first find out if Joan has gone to the cave. Wait a minute. Tibby, fetch me the magic basin."

Tibby, the little round cat, at once

got up and fetched a basin from a shelf. She filled it with blue water from a jug, and set it on a stool in front of Roundy. He took a peacock's feather and stroked the water gently, whispering a string of magic words all the time, which neither Billy nor Tom could understand. Suddenly the water became still and flat like a mirror. Roundy bent over it and breathed on it. Then he rubbed it clean with a duster.

"Look!" he said. "You can see your sister now!"

Billy and Tom looked into the basin of blue water, and on the mirror-like surface they saw a picture. In the middle was Joan, very tiny, still walking with the blue shoes on her feet. As they watched, she came to a little door in a hillside. It swung open and she walked through a long, long passage, which got darker and darker. Then suddenly she came to a cave, and there in the middle sat Candle-Shoe, the old, ugly magician.

Just at that moment the water seemed to cloud over, and the wonderful pictures vanished. Billy and Tom looked at Roundy in despair, for they could not bear to think of poor Joan in the power of that old magician.

"Yes, it's what I thought," said Roundy, emptying the water out of the window. "Candle-Shoe has got her. Well, how are we going to rescue her?"

"First of all, where is this cave?" asked Tom.

"Nobody knows," said Roundy.

"But how can we go there, then?" asked Billy.

"Let me think for a moment." said Roundy. He sat down on a stool, put his head in his hands and frowned hard. Then he suddenly snapped his fingers, and jumped up.

"I've got it! Look here, we'll find another pair of old Candle-Shoe's shoes and put them on. They will lead us to the cave, and we shall know just where it is."

"Yes, but the shoes go so fast that whoever is following can't keep up," said Tom.

"Ah," said Roundy, "but I can tell you what to do about that! We'll only put *one* shoe on, and then we shall go slowly enough for us all to keep up. I'll put the shoe on, and you shall follow me."

"But how shall we find out where a pair of the shoes has been put?" said Billy. "We can't go looking in every hollow tree."

"Oh, that's easy enough," said Roundy. "My house will take us to a pair in a twinkling."

"Your house!" said Billy and Tom together. "But how can a house do that?"

"Well, you see, it's quite round," said the little man, smiling. "It can roll along like a ball, and that's how I get about all over the world."

"But what about the chimney?" asked Billy. "That sticks out, you know."

Roundy opened the door and went

outside the house. The boys followed him. He gave a big jump and landed just beside the chimney. He pressed hard on it and it sank down into the house, leaving just a hole where it had stood before. The boys were too surprised to say a word.

"Ha," said Roundy, jumping down again. "Mine's a fine little house, isn't it? Now would you like to come inside while my house rolls along, or would you rather follow it, walking behind?"

"Oh, I think we'd rather follow it," said Tom. "We should be so dreadfully bumped about inside, shouldn't we? What about you, Roundy? Do you stay inside when your house goes travelling?"

"Oh yes," said Roundy. "I don't get hurt because I'm quite round, you see. I just roll about like a ball, and so does Tibby. Now wait a moment . . . I want to tell the house where to go."

Roundy leaned against his round house and stroked it as if it were a cat – and to Billy's surprise, and Tom's, it began to purr!

"Little house, little house," said Roundy in a loving voice. "Do you know where Candle-Shoe hides his pairs of shoes?"

The house purred more loudly than ever.

"You do?" said Roundy. "That's good. Then take me to one of those pairs of shoes, little house."

He popped inside, and slammed the door. The house suddenly began to roll itself away through the wood, just like a great big ball. Billy and Tom stared and stared – it looked very strange indeed. They followed it. It didn't go very fast, and all the time it rolled it seemed to be humming a song. It was the funniest house the boys had ever seen.

It rolled through the wood, and came to the open country. Then it came to a shallow river and bounced into the water. Billy and Tom jumped in too and paddled across behind the big ball of a house. The house rolled up the bank of the opposite side and stopped. The door flew open and out came Roundy with a duster.

"I must just dry it before it gets a chill," he said to the boys. "Sit in the hot sun for a few minutes, you two, and your feet will soon be dry."

The boys sat down and dried their feet, whilst Roundy rubbed and polished his funny little house. Then he popped indoors again, and the house rolled on once more.

It rolled until it came to a green hillside. It came to a stop beside a bramble bush. The door flew open and out ran Roundy.

"There must be a pair of shoes somewhere here," he said in excitement. So they all looked hard — and sure enough, Tom soon came across them. They were red this time, quite small, and had silver buckles just like the others.

"Ha!" said Roundy, taking them from

Tom. "Now I'll just put one on!"

He popped one on his right foot, and held out his hands to Billy and Tom.

"The magic's working!" he said. "Come on! My house will follow too. It always goes where I go."

The boys each took one of Roundy's fat hands, and went with him. The house followed behind, humming its strange little song.

"You see, wearing only one of the shoes means that I don't go at all fast," said Roundy.

The shoe took him up the hill to the top, and then down the other side. There was a deep pit at the foot of the hill, and a flight of stone steps led down to the bottom. Down went Roundy, and the two boys scrambled behind. At the bottom of the pit was a large trap-door which opened as they came near. They went through it, and saw more steps leading downwards. Soon they were in a long dark passage, lighted here and there by tiny lamps. Down they went and down, right into the heart of the earth – and then up they came, and up, until at last they could see daylight ahead of them once more.

When they came out of the passage into the sunshine they saw in front of them a very steep mountain.

"That must be the mountain the magician lives in," said Billy to Tom. They made their way towards it, and saw a narrow winding path. The magic shoe took Roundy up and up, and at last the three of them saw a door in the hillside, fast shut.

"Hold me whilst I slip off this shoe," said Roundy. "I don't want to walk into the cave just yet!"

The two boys held tight whilst Roundy pulled off the magic shoe. He tossed it away, and put on his own. Then he sat down and looked round.

"Well, we're here," he said. "The next thing to decide is – how are we going to rescue Joan?"

They all thought for five minutes — and then Roundy began to chuckle.

"I think I know," he said. "I'll just play a nice little trick on old Candle-Shoe. You two hide yourselves and watch."

The boys went behind a bush and peeped out to see what Roundy meant to do. He went boldly to the door in the mountainside and knocked loudly seven times. In a moment the door swung open and the magician himself looked out.

"What do you want?" he said crossly. "Go away or I'll turn you into a grasshopper."

"I beg your pardon," said Roundy, bowing to the ground. "But see, Your Highness, I have brought a marvellous house for you to see. Maybe you would like to buy it."

The magician looked at the round house which at once hummed its song again and turned itself about for Candle-Shoe to see. The magician was astonished.

He put on a pair of enormous spectacles and walked over to the house.

"This is a strange affair," he said to Roundy. "Never in my life have I seen a house like this."

"It follows its owner like a dog," said Roundy. "It will always come if you whistle. It has a pull-out chimney, and a little round cat to sit by the fire."

Roundy pulled the chimney out and pushed it in to show the magician, who was more astonished than ever.

"Now buy it, sir, do," said Roundy. "Think what a surprise it will be to all your friends, the witches, and think how they will envy you."

"How much is it?" asked the magician.

"Only four gold pieces," said Roundy.

"It seems very cheap," said Candle-Shoe in surprise. "Is there anything wrong with it inside?"

"No, Your Highness," said Roundy. "Please go in and look around."

The magician pushed open the door and stepped inside. Roundy gave a great shout of joy, and slammed the door at once. He locked it, and then gave his house a push.

"Roll up and down the mountainside!" he commanded. "Give the old magician a shake-up, little house!"

At once the house began to roll up the hill and down, and the magician inside began to yell and shout in fright. Roundy took no notice, and he and the two boys rushed into the cave and began to look for Joan. They went down a long dark passage and soon came to the place where Joan was, for they could hear her calling.

But alas! The door was locked! Billy banged on it and called to Joan.

"Joanie! Joanie!" he shouted. "Are you all right?"

"Oh, Billy!" cried Joan's voice. "Have you come to rescue me? Yes, I'm all right, but I've been frightened because that horrid old magician wanted me to help him with his spells and I wouldn't."

"Where's the key to this door?" asked Tom.

"Oh, the magician has got it hanging on his belt," said Joan. "However can you get it?"

The three outside the door looked at one another in dismay.

"Come on," said Roundy to Billy. "We'll go and see if we can get it, somehow or other. You stay here and keep Joan cheerful, Tom."

Off went Billy and Roundy. They came out on the hillside and looked to see what the little house was doing. It was still rolling up and down and the magician was still calling and shouting for help.

"Stop, little house," said Roundy. The house stopped, and stood still. Roundy ran up to it.

He called to the magician. "Throw your keys out of the window, quickly."

"Certainly not!" said the magician, angrily. "I'm not going to let you have that little girl back again!"

"Little house, roll faster!" commanded Roundy. At once the little house began to roll around faster than ever and Candle-Shoe was bumped about inside in a dreadful manner. He begged for mercy, and Roundy stopped the little house again.

"Where are those keys?" he cried. The magician threw them out of the window, and Roundy picked them up in glee.

"Go on little house, roll around a little more so that Candle-Shoe can't get out!" he said, and the house began to roll about gently.

Billy and Roundy ran back through the dark passage to the cave. Roundy fitted the biggest key in the lock and turned it. The door opened and Joan ran out. Billy and Tom hugged her tightly, and Joan began to cry for joy. Then the boys told her who Roundy was, and she hugged the little man too.

"How will we get back?" said Tom.

"Let's look about in the magician's cave," said Roundy. "We are sure to find something or other that will take you back safely."

They looked here and they looked there, and suddenly Roundy gave a shout of joy.

"Here's a witch's broomstick," he cried. "We'll take it outside, and if you all sit on it and wish yourselves home you'll be there in half a shake of a duck's tail!"

"But what about you?" asked Billy, as they ran outside into the sunshine.

"You'll see what happens to me when you're safely in the air on your broomstick!" laughed Roundy. "Hop on!"

They all sat on the broomstick, and then Roundy suddenly clapped his hands twice and called out a magic word. The children wished themselves home, and up in the air rose the broomstick at once. The riders held tight, and looked down to see the last of Roundy.

He commanded the little house to stop rolling, and unlocked the door. At once the magician leapt out — but before he could get hold of Roundy, that fat little man had hopped inside the door, banged it shut, and the little house was scurrying away down the mountainside as fast as an express train!

How the children laughed to see it!

"Hurray for Roundy!" said Billy. "He was a good friend to us! I do hope we see him again some day!"

Their broomstick flew faster and faster, and at last brought them right over their own house. It flew down into the garden, and the three children jumped off. Billy put out his hand to catch the broomstick and take it indoors to show his mother but he wasn't quite quick enough — for it flew away from him, and rose up into the air once more.

"There it goes!" said Joan. "Oh, what an adventure we've had. Quick, let's go in and tell Mummy before we forget anything!"

Sly-One buys his apples

There was once a rascally brownie called Sly-One, who bought fine red apples at a penny each, and sold them at a penny each, too. Now you might think that that was a silly thing to do, because he wouldn't make any money for himself – but he did! He became very rich, and all the brownies thought that there really must be some magic about his buying and selling.

Now one day I happened to be near when Sly-One was buying his apples from the Apple-Woman who lives down Cuckoo Lane. He was counting them out from a tub and putting them on to his barrow, and I could see and hear plainly what he was doing. He wanted fifty apples, and as I watched him, he began counting them.

"One, two, three, four, five, six, seven, eight, nine," he counted aloud. "My, Apple-Woman, there's a fine red apple for you! It's so red it reminds me of the cheeks of that little girl who lives down Cradle Valley. She's a bonny little thing, and only five years old, too! Yes, only five! Five, six, seven, eight, nine, ten, eleven, twelve, thirteen, fourteen, fifteen – hey! Is that one of your hens got loose? Look, there it is running over the road. How many hens have you got, Apple-Woman? Twelve! My, that's a fine lot, isn't it? Twelve! Twelve, thirteen, fourteen, fifteen, sixteen, seventeen, eighteen, nineteen, twenty, twenty-one, twenty-two – oh, excuse me, I'm going to sneeze!"

Sly-One took out his handkerchief and did a most tremendous sneeze.

"A-tishoo! A-TISHOO!" he sneezed. Then he put his handkerchief away again.

"The other day I sneezed twenty times running!" he told the Apple-Woman. "Twenty! Just think of it. Twenty, twenty-one, twenty-two, twenty-three, twenty-four, twenty-five, twenty-six, twenty-seven, and twenty-eight, twenty-nine, thirty, thirty-one, thirty-two, thirty-three, thirty-four – that's the number of your little house, Apple-Woman, isn't it? Now, I live at number thirty-one. Thirty-one, thirty-two, and thirty-three, thirty-four, thirty-five, thirty-six, thirty-seven, thirty-eight, and thirty-nine, forty, forty-one, forty-two, forty-three, forty-four, forty-five, forty-six – that reminds me, Apple-Woman, there were forty-six rooks in my garden yesterday – what do you think of that? And the day before that there were forty-two! Forty-two! Forty-three, forty-four, forty-five . . ."

Now I wonder if you can see the trick that Sly-One was playing on the poor old Apple-Woman. She listened to him talking, and saw him taking out the apples one by one, and she didn't know that although he seemed to be counting them very carefully, he was taking far more than he should.

He went on counting. "Forty-five, forty-six, forty-seven, forty-eight – that's how old I am, Apple-Woman – forty-eight last birthday. My, how the time does fly, doesn't it? It seems only the other day that I was forty-one, yes, surely, it does. Forty-one! Forty-two, forty-three, forty-four, forty-five, forty-six, forty-seven, forty-eight, forty-nine – do you know, Apple-Woman, I have got forty-nine buttons on my new coat – no, I'm wrong. I lost one yesterday, so there's only forty-eight now. Yes, forty-eight. Forty-eight, forty-nine, fifty!"

He put the last apple on his barrow, and paid the Apple-Woman fifty pence for them. Then he politely said good morning, raised his pointed cap, and wheeled his barrow away.

Do you know how many apples the old rascal had on his gaily painted barrow?

He had eighty-three, for which he had only paid fifty pence. The Apple-Woman thought that her apple-tub looked rather empty, but as she had heard the brownie counting the apples, she thought it must be all right.

Now not long after that I happened to pass by Sly-One's cottage, and I saw him selling fifty apples to a customer who had bought a bag in which to take them away. I stopped and listened to him selling them, and this is how he sold them.

"You want fifty apples, Pippitty," he said. "Very well, I have some fine ones here. I'll count them out for you, if you'll hold out your bag. Now then — one, two, three, four, five, six, seven, eight — how's your sister, Pippitty? — she wasn't at all well when I saw her last. Oh, I'm glad she's better. Let me see, how many sisters and brothers have you got? Fifteen! My, that's a great number! Fifteen! Fifteen, sixteen, seventeen, eighteen, nineteen, twenty,

twenty-one – by the way, did you know that the Queen is going to have twenty-one fiddlers at the next dance? Yes, she is, really. There was a talk about having thirty-one! Fancy that! Thirty-one!"

Sly-One popped the apples into the bag as he talked, and his customer listened to him.

"Thirty-one, thirty-two, thirty-three, thirty-four – have you heard that poor old Raggedy the Gnome has been turned out of the cottage he's lived in for thirty-four years?" asked Sly-One. "Yes, thirty-four years he's lived there, and he told me, poor old chap, that he had hoped to live there for *forty-eight* years. But he won't now. Forty-eight, forty-nine, fifty. There, that's the lot. Have you brought your fifty pennies with you?"

Pippitty had, and he handed them over to Sly-One. Then he went off with his bag, thinking that he had got fifty fine red apples in it. Hadn't he heard Sly-One count them?

But alas for poor old Pippitty! He had only got twenty-two!

And it's no wonder that Sly-One gets rich, is it? For he had got back the fifty pennies he had spent that morning, and on his barrow he still had sixty-one apples left to sell!

But that sort of thing really can't be allowed, so tomorrow I am going to the Apple-Woman, and I shall ask her if she will let *me* count her apples out to Sly-One when he comes to buy them. I shall play his own trick on him – and I do wonder what he'll do, don't you?

The boy on the bicycle

Mummy was telling the two children what to buy that morning. She was ill in bed, so she couldn't do any shopping or work.

Jane had cleaned up the little house as best she could, and Will had brought in some wood and coal for the fire. Now they were to go and do the shopping.

Jane looked down at the list of things. "I wish we could buy some eggs for you and some fruit, Mummy," she said. "The doctor said you were to have them, you know. But you haven't put them down on the list."

"There isn't money enough for them, dear," said her mother. "So I must do without. I'm lucky to have two children like you that I can trust. I'd rather have that than eggs and fruit."

"I'd like you to have *both*," said Will. He fetched the basket and the two set off to the town. It was Saturday morning and very busy. Cars swept by, and errand boys on bicycles darted here and there.

Suddenly there came a cry. "Look out, there! You'll have an accident!"

The two children looked round. Down the hill came a boy on a bicycle at top speed. He seemed to have forgotten that he had any brakes to put on. He swung round the corner by Jane without putting his hand out to warn traffic. A car pulled up quickly and almost ran on to the pavement.

The boy fell off his bicycle, sat up in the road and howled. He had bruised his arm, grazed his hands and hurt his knees.

Will picked up his bicycle, which had the front wheel bent. Jane picked up the boy and dusted him down. People came round to see if he was all right, but finding that two children were seeing to him, and that he wasn't much hurt, they went away again. But the man in the car called out crossly: "Don't you come out on your bike again till you've learnt the rules of the road."

The boy was still crying. "Cheer up," said Will. "You're not hurt much. We'll take you home. Where do you live?"

"At the Big House," said the boy, pointing up the hill. "We've only just come, about two weeks ago. Oh, my poor knee!"

"It just wants bathing," said Jane. "Come along up the hill. Will can wheel your bike. Your mother can bathe your knee and bandage it."

"I want you to bathe my knee," said the boy. "My name's Mike. What's yours?"

Wiping away his tears, the boy walked up the hill with Jane and Will, telling them about his new house and the lovely garden.

"There are peaches in the greenhouse," he said. "And plums on the trees all purple and ripe. And we are going to have thousands of apples and pears."

"You're lucky," said Jane. "We have just one fruit tree in our garden, and that's an apple tree that never has any apples!"

They turned in at a big gateway and walked up the drive. It was so big that Jane felt rather scared. "I don't think we'd better come any farther," she said.

"Yes, come to my playroom," said Mike. "You said you'd bathe my knee for me. I don't want my mother to."

"Why not?" said Jane. "I always like my mother to see to me if I'm hurt."

They came to a big playroom with a garden door. They went in. There was a basin with hot and cold water at one end, and Jane went to it. She found a flannel and began to bathe Mike's knee gently.

Mike began to boast. "Did you see me

come down the hill at top speed? I'm not allowed to go out of the garden, really! Not till I'm more used to my bike. I've only had it three days. Mummy said I wasn't to go into the village yet."

Jane stopped bathing Mike's knee. She looked up at him.

"Well, your mother was quite right. See what a nasty little accident you had! You came down that hill without even putting your brakes on. You might have fallen right under that car. Your mother will be upset when she hears."

"She won't hear," said Mike. "I shan't tell her. She'll think I fell off my bike in the garden. I keep lots of things from my mother."

"Then I think you deserve to have an accident," said Will, in disgust. "Here you've got a lovely house and a gorgeous garden, and a new bike, and a sensible, kind mother – and you go off and disobey her and then say you're going to deceive her. Come on, Jane. Don't bother about his knee. He's not worth bringing home and making a fuss about!"

There was a movement at the end of the room and a man came forward. It was Mike's father. He had been there all the time!

"I was watching you two kind children," he said, "and I couldn't help hearing all you said. You are quite right to talk to Mike like that. He needs friends like you! He's a spoilt, disobedient little boy, who doesn't know how lucky he is."

"Well – he is lucky," said Jane, going red. "We've only got a little cottage – and our mother is ill, and we can't even get her the eggs and fruit the doctor says she ought to have. We're looking after her as best we can. We wouldn't dream of being silly like Mike, and upsetting her by having an accident because we were stupid and deceitful."

"You hear that, Mike?" said his father. "Now you see what sensible, good-hearted children think of you when you boast of being disobedient and deceitful. I hope you're ashamed of yourself. These are the sort of children who would make very fine friends for you – but I'm sure that now they won't want to see you again."

Mike looked as if he was going to burst into tears again. He caught hold of Jane's hand. "I was just boasting," he said. "I'd look after my mother, too, if she was ill. I'm sorry about yours. Daddy, can I get some eggs from the hen-house and some peaches and plums and take them to Jane's mother? And, please, Jane and Will, come and see me again. I haven't got any friends here."

Jane was delighted to hear about the eggs and the fruit. Just what Mummy ought to have. She smiled at Mike. "Perhaps you're not so bad as you sound," she said. "If your father likes, we *will* come and see you again, and play with you."

"And put a bit of your common sense and kindness into his head," said Mike's father. "I'd like you to do that. Come along; we'll get the eggs. And when your mother can spare you, come and play with Mike, and stay to tea."

That was how Jane and Will became friends with Mike, up at the Big House. Mike learnt a lot from them, and in return he gave them the eggs and fruit their mother needed, so that she soon got better.

Will has taught him the rules of the road and now Mike is allowed to go out on his bicycle by himself into the town. Very often he lends it to Will and Jane — and how grand they feel pedalling along to do the shopping!

They don't know it yet, but Mike's father and mother are giving them bicycles on their next birthdays. Won't it be a fine surprise!

The bear with button eyes

There was once a little teddy bear who had button eyes. He could see quite well with them, but he couldn't shut them to go to sleep. He didn't mind this a bit because he was always very wide awake.

Now one day, Mollie, his little mistress, took him out into the garden to play, and suddenly a dreadful thing happened. One of his button eyes came loose, and dropped into the grass! How upset the little bear was!

Mollie didn't notice it. She was setting out her tea set, and didn't see that the bear had only one eye. He did his best to show her, but she went on playing tea-parties, and didn't look at him.

"Oh my, oh my!" thought the little bear, "what am I to do? I am going to a dance with all the other toys tonight, and I can't go with only one eye!"

Then Mollie heard her mother calling her to come in and she quickly put her toys away and ran indoors, taking the teddy with her. The bear couldn't think *what* he was to do! He really *must* get his eye back before the dance that night!

He sat in the toy cupboard, very sad and quiet. His friend the bunny-rabbit wondered what was the matter.

"What is making you so sad?" he asked, putting a soft paw into the teddy bear's brown one.

"One of my button eyes fell out on to the grass," said the bear, sadly. "Mollie didn't notice, and I am sure I don't know how I can go to a dance with only one eye. What am I to do?"

The bunny thought hard. Then he squeezed the bear's paw.

"As soon as it is night and the moon

is up, I will take all the toy soldiers into the garden and they shall look for your button eye," he said.

"Oh, thank you," said the bear, very gratefully.

So as soon as Mollie had gone to bed, and the moon was up, the bunny-rabbit made all the toy soldiers march out of their fortress and follow him into the garden. Then they looked and looked and looked for the button eye.

But they couldn't find it! It was most surprising. It wasn't anywhere in the garden at all.

A little brownie came running by, and he stopped in astonishment to see so many toy soldiers about.

"Whatever are you doing here?" he asked.

"Looking for teddy bear's button eye," said the rabbit. "He dropped it here this afternoon, and he says he can't go to our dance tonight without it."

"Good gracious!" said the brownie. "I

know what has happened to it!"

"What?" asked all the soldiers and the bunny together.

"Why, Fairy Littlefeet came by this evening," said the brownie, "and she had lost a black button from her right shoe. Suddenly she saw one in the grass, and she picked it up and sewed it on to her shoe. I lent her a needle and thread myself."

"Oh my!" said the bunny in dismay. "Now what are we to do? Do you know where Littlefeet lives?"

"No," said the brownie. "I don't. I'm afraid the bear won't get his button eye back now."

Everyone was quite quiet, thinking what to do. Then at last the brownie spoke.

"If only you could get another button from somewhere, I could perhaps sew it on for you myself," he said.

The bunny thanked him very much.

"There may be one in Mollie's work-basket," he said. "I'll go and see."

So he and all the soldiers went back into the playroom again and hunted in Mollie's work-basket. But there were only pearl buttons there, and those wouldn't do for eyes. The bunny was in despair. What could he do for the teddy bear? It was getting nearly time to start the dance, and he did so badly want his friend to go.

Then he thought of a splendid idea. He knew that Mollie wore shoes with buttons on. If only he could find those, perhaps he could cut one off, and that would do splendidly for the bear.

So he hurried to the boot cupboard. But Mollie's black shoes had gone to be mended, and there was only a white pair there, with white buttons on.

"Perhaps a white button would do just as well," thought the bunny. "I expect he could see with it all right."

So he took a pair of scissors and snipped the button from one shoe. Then he ran to the bear.

"Come along," he said. "I've got a button that will do for you. It's white, but I'm sure it won't matter."

He took him to the brownie, and the little man fetched a reel of spider thread and a pine needle. In a trice he had sewn on the white boot button, and the teddy bear had two eyes!

"I can see beautifully!" he said, looking all round. "That is splendid! Do I look very funny?"

He did look a bit odd with one white eye and one black one, but the bunny told him that he looked lovely. So off he went to the dance feeling very happy.

Now in the morning Mollie went to put her white shoes on – and wasn't she surprised to find the button gone!

"Why, both buttons were there when I put them away yesterday," she said. "Where can the other one be?"

Then she suddenly caught sight of the teddy bear, staring at her with his one black button eye and his one white one. She ran to him and picked him up.

"Oh, you poor darling!" she cried. "How did you get that white button for an eye? You had two black ones yesterday! The fairies must have come in the night and sewn it on for you!"

Mollie looked at it carefully and saw that it was most beautifully sewn on with spider thread instead of cotton. Then she knew for certain that some fairy had been at work, and she was filled with delight.

"Now I know there are fairies!" she cried. "Oh, Teddy, you shall keep your white eye to remind me. I do wish you could tell me what had happened!"

But he never did tell her. He still has one white and one black button for eyes, so if ever you meet him you are sure to know him!

The boy who threw stones

There was no boy in the school who could throw better than Jock. He could throw a ball higher and farther than any other boy, and he could throw stones at anything and hit it, smack in the middle.

But he threw stones far too much. He threw them at animals and he threw them at birds. He didn't throw them at the other boys, because they punished him if he did.

"You keep your stones to yourself," said Peter, fiercely. "And let me tell you this, Jock – it's a cowardly thing to do, to throw stones at dogs and cats and birds, as you do. So just stop doing it."

But Jock couldn't stop. He always

carried a pocketful of round stones, and his hand was always in his pocket, choosing a stone to throw at the next animal or bird he saw.

When the grown-ups found out what an unpleasant habit he had, they were cross with him. So Jock gave up throwing stones when the grown-ups were about. He took walks by himself in the fields, and practised throwing stones at animals and birds there.

He threw stones at the cows and made them gallop about the field in

fright. He threw them at the sheep and they herded together in alarm. He threw them at the geese and hit one on the leg. It limped badly after that.

A small girl saw him. She called indignantly after him.

"You're a cruel boy! Stop throwing stones. One day you'll be sorry!"

"Pooh! You sound like a grown-up!" said Jock, and threw another stone, this time at a freckled thrush.

"Well, grown-ups and children think the same about a lot of things!" called the little girl. "You *will* be sorry one day!"

Jock saw a moorhen on the nearby river and sent a stone after it. He almost hit it. The little thing cried out "crek-crek!" in alarm, sank itself under the water and swam away quickly.

He threw a stone at a pretty wild duck, standing preening its feathers by the side of the water. The stone struck the duck hard on its right leg – and the duck's leg was broken!

It gave a terrified quack and flew into the air, the broken leg dangling down in a strange way.

"Oh! You wicked boy! You've broken that duck's leg!" cried the little girl, and she ran up to him and pummelled him hard, she was so upset. Jock pushed her away.

"Stop it! That was a jolly good shot of mine! Hit it bang on the leg."

"Oh, you hateful boy! That poor duck will have to put up with only one good leg for the rest of its life!" wept the little girl. "It can't go to a doctor. It doesn't know what has happened. Oh, look – it's flown down again – it's trying to stand on its poor broken leg as well as its good one. It doesn't know what has happened to it – poor, poor creature!"

"You're a silly little softy, going on about a stupid duck like that," said Jock, and he walked away whistling.

The next Saturday, he went walking by the river again, his pocket full of stones as usual. And, swimming near the water's edge, he saw a young swan – a cygnet. Out came a stone, and Jock sent it skimming so near the cygnet that it almost hit it.

But what was this? What was this enormous white creature suddenly coming up the bank towards him? Jock stood and stared.

It was the father of the cygnet, a big, powerful swan, gleaming white. It had seen Jock, and knew that he had tried to hurt the cygnet. So, fierce in defence of its young one, as all parent swans are, it had come to warn Jock off.

Jock laughed at the big waddling bird. He flipped a stone at it. And then something happened. The swan came right up to Jock, lifted one of its powerful wings and struck the boy on his right arm.

"Oh! Oh! You've hurt me!" shouted Jock, in great pain. He looked at his arm. He couldn't seem to use it. "You've broken my arm! You hateful creature! Oh, my arm, my arm!"

The swan had certainly broken Jock's arm. There was no doubt about that. The big bird went back to the river and swam away with its cygnet. Jock was left howling by the water. Then he heard a voice behind him.

It was the little girl again. "I saw all that happened. You're the boy who broke that duck's leg last week, aren't you? And today you tried to hit that cygnet. So the big swan came after you – and broke your arm!"

"Oh!" wept Jock. "What shall I do?"

"You can come home with me," said the little girl. "My father's a doctor. He can set your arm for you so that it will mend again – but nobody has set that poor duck's leg. You don't deserve help. You're a cruel boy and I don't like you – but I'll take you home to my father."

Still sobbing, Jock went with the little girl to her father's house. Soon the doctor was examining the broken arm. The little girl told him the story of how Jock came to get it.

The doctor looked stern. "Look here, my lad," he said, "if I don't mend your arm, you will never, never be able to throw stones at anything again, because your arm will be of no use to you. You have caused a great deal of harm and pain to other creatures. Can you tell me why I should mend your arm? Why should you have an arm that does so much damage? Look at my right arm and my hand. Do you know what I use them for?"

Jock didn't answer. He was feeling terribly ashamed of himself.

"I'll tell you," said the doctor. "I use this hand and arm to help those who are sick and ill, whose limbs are broken and damaged. I use it to help those who come to me in pain for help and comfort. That is what I use my arm for. You know what you use yours for. Now, just tell me – why should I mend it?"

"Oh, please do, sir," begged Jock. "I know what it feels like now to be in pain and to have a useless limb. I've had a dreadful lesson. I shan't be able to play cricket, or swim, or do anything much for a long time – but when my arm is mended, I promise you I'll never use it to harm others again. I'll only use it for good things. I promise you, sir."

The doctor set the bones of Jock's arm. Then he took him home in his car. He left him at his door, with a stern face.

"Your own doctor will see to you now," he said. "But I shall keep my eye on you, boy. My little girl was right when she said you would be sorry some day. You're sorry now – but if you're not sorry enough to keep your promise and mend your ways, you'll certainly be sorrier still in the future."

But Jock *is* keeping his promise. There are never any stones in his pockets now. He's a much nicer boy. He would really like to be friends with the doctor's little girl, but she won't be friends – yet. You see, she can't forget that duck's poor broken leg.

It grew and it grew

Once little Fibs, the pixie, told his mother a story. He often didn't tell the truth, and it made her sad.

Fibs had been playing with his ball in the garden and it had gone on to the rose-bed. He had gone to get it and had trodden all over the bed and broken some roses off.

"Oh, Fibs – did *you* do that?" cried his mother.

"No. It was Frisky, the dog," said Fibs.

"Then he's very naughty," said his mother. "Go and find him and tie him up."

Fibs didn't want to do that. He liked Frisky. But he ran out and pretended to look for him. "Mother, he's frightened and he's gone into the next door garden," he said, when he came back. That was another fib, of course. That first fib was certainly growing!

"Oh dear!" said his mother in dismay. "Dame Pitpat has hens, and if Frisky chases them she will be so cross. Go and ask her if she will let you go into her garden and catch him."

Fibs ran off. He went next door and pretended to ring the bell. Nobody came, of course, because he *hadn't* rung the bell. He ran back to his mother.

"Dame Pitpat is out," he said. "I rang and I rang, and nobody came. But never mind – Frisky ran out of her garden and he's gone down the road."

"Well, that's good," said his mother. "But I shall certainly tie him up when he comes in."

She went into the garden to hang up some clothes. Fibs heaved a sigh of relief. Perhaps now he needn't tell another fib.

Soon his mother came hurrying in. "Fibs, Fibs, where are you? There's a burglar in Dame Pitpat's house. There must be, because you said she was out. I distinctly saw someone at the upstairs window. You go and ask old Rappy to come along and find out!"

Fibs sighed. Oh dear, oh dear! It was all beginning again! He ran out to Mr Rappy's house, but he didn't knock at the door. He just stood there – then he went back again to his mother.

"Mr Rappy says he's got a very bad leg and he can't come. He says you must have been mistaken. There can't be a burglar in Dame Pitpat's house."

"How does *he* know?" cried his mother. "Well, I shall send you to Mr Plod, the policeman, then. *Somebody* must come and get the burglar next door! Run, Fibs, run and get Mr Plod at once."

Fibs couldn't think *what* to do! He was standing there, wondering what to say, when his mother gave a loud cry. "Oh! There *is* Mr Plod! Look, by the front gate. Go and get him at once!"

Fibs went out slowly, hoping that Mr Plod would have gone by the time he reached the gate. His mother ran out crossly. "Why don't you hurry, Fibs? Mr Plod, Mr Plod! There's a robber in Dame Pitpat's house!"

Mr Plod turned in surprise. "Is there really, Ma'am? Then I'll climb in at a window and catch him right away!"

And in no time at all there was Mr Plod climbing in at a window of Dame Pitpat's house! There was nobody downstairs so he went upstairs very quietly and walked into the bedroom.

Somebody screamed and sat up in bed! It was Dame Pitpat herself, having a little rest. "Oh, what is it? Who is it? Why, it's Mr Plod! What do you want, Mr Plod?"

"Well, I was told there was a burglar in the house," said Mr Plod. "Little Fibs next door was sent to you with a message and he came back and said

you were out, and then his mother saw somebody moving in the upstairs room, and . . ."

"Bless us all! I wasn't out!" said Dame Pitpat. "He couldn't have rung the bell or I'd have heard it. It was me that Fibs' mother saw upstairs. Please go away, Mr Plod, and leave me in peace."

Mr Plod went down and told Fibs' mother and she was really very puzzled. She was even more puzzled when she saw Mr Rappy coming out of his house with his stick under his arm, walking quickly to catch the bus.

"Why, Mr Rappy! When Fibs asked you for help just now, you told him you couldn't come because you had a very bad leg!" cried Fibs' mother, looking very amazed.

"Nonsense!" said Mr Rappy. "He never came to ask me anything at all. Just one of his tales!" He rapped with his stick on the fence. "He wants a taste of this – then he wouldn't tell so many stories!"

"Fibs! You didn't go to Mr Rappy – and I don't believe you went to Dame Pitpat's either!" said his mother, shocked. "And I don't suppose Frisky was in her garden. Where *is* he then? Frisky, Frisky!"

A loud barking came from upstairs. Fibs' mother ran up and opened a door. Inside the room was Frisky, wagging his tail.

"Why, he's been here all the time," said Fibs' mother. "He's been asleep on his rug. He *couldn't* have run over the bed and broken the roses. Then who did, Fibs? Answer me that!"

She went out to the bed – and there she saw the footprints quite clearly. They were Fibs', of course.

"You horrid mean little pixie!" she cried. "Blaming poor Frisky – telling me he had run away next door – and saying that Dame Pitpat was out and Mr Rappy had a bad leg. Don't you know that one fib leads to another and always brings trouble in the end? Well, trouble is coming to *you*, Fibs!"

Poor Fibs! His mother told the truth – it was ages before he was allowed out to play again. It's strange how one fib leads to another, isn't it? Fibs knows that now and he'll never forget it!

Mr Stamp-About in a fix

"I've written three times to Mr Tiles to tell him to come and mend my roof!" said Mr Stamp-About to his sister. "And what does he say? He says he's too busy! Pah! Too busy to mend *my* roof! Just wait till I see him!"

"Please don't stamp on that rug," said his sister. "You're making the dust fly about. I think it's because you're so bad-tempered that people won't come and do things for you. Now stop stamping. If you *want* to beat the dust out of that rug, take it out, hang it over the line and beat it."

"Pah!" said Mr Stamp-About, and stalked out of the room. He put on his hat and went to find Mr Tiles. He found

him in a shed, getting together his tools to go and do a job.

Mr Stamp-About caught hold of him. "Ha! I suppose you were just about to come and mend my roof! Now don't you dare to say you weren't! You come along with me this minute!"

Little Mr Tiles looked at the big, fierce Mr Stamp-About. "Let go," he said. "If you force me to go with you like this I'll have to come – but I won't put your tiles on properly, so there!"

"Oh, yes, you will!" said Mr Stamp-About. "Because I'll sit by you and watch you! And not a penny will you get if you don't do your best work. Now bring some tiles along with you, and a pot of paint, too, to touch up the gutters. And I shall sit on a chimney-pot and watch you!"

"You will, will you?" said little Mr Tiles. "Right. I'll get the tiles – here they are. And I'll bring this pot and this brush along with me. Off we go!"

And off they went together,

Mr Stamp-About holding on fast to Mr Tiles in case he ran off. But he didn't. He walked along quite amiably, and talked about the weather.

"Fetch the ladder," said Mr Stamp-About, when they got to his house. "It's in my shed. Climb up it first and begin to put on the new tiles. I'm going to have a cup of hot cocoa as it's a cold day. Then I'll come up the ladder, and sit on a chimney-pot to watch you. I'll have a fine view of your work, I can tell you!"

Mr Tiles went to fetch the ladder. He set it up against the gutter and climbed up. Mr Stamp-About had disappeared into the house to get his cocoa. Dear, dear – he hadn't even thought of offering cold Mr Tiles a cup. Still, that suited Mr Tiles all right. He had something to do before Mr Stamp-About came out again!

He climbed the ladder quickly, taking his tiles with him. He set them down on the roof and then went back for his pot and his brush. He grinned as he brought those up. He took a quick look down. Mr Stamp-About was nowhere to be seen. He was somewhere in the house, having cocoa and biscuits!

Mr Tiles looked at the two chimneys sticking up out of the roof. One was smoking. One wasn't, so that was the one that Mr Stamp-About would sit on to watch Mr Tiles doing his work! Aha!

Mr Tiles climbed up to the chimney-pot. It was squat and round. He took his brush and dipped it into his pot. He painted the rim of the pot round and round and round.

But not with paint. Oh, no! There was no paint in that pot – there was glue. Nice, sticky glue! Aha, Mr Stamp-About, you didn't know that, did you, because the pot was labelled "White Paint"!

Mr Tiles grinned. He slid down to where the roof needed new tiles and set to work. Presently he heard Mr Stamp-About climbing up the ladder. He saw him clambering up to the chimney-pot and sitting himself flat down on it, just as if it were a stool. Mr Tiles grinned to himself.

"Now, get on, Tiles," said Stamp-About. "I can see everything you do. You're to work well and quickly. I'm not going to pay you too much, either."

"You're going to pay me twenty pounds," said Mr Tiles. "Or your sister is. Twenty pounds, Mr Stamp-About — part-payment for this work, and part-payment for your bad temper!"

If Mr Stamp-About hadn't been stuck fast to the chimney-pot he would have fallen off in rage. He stamped his feet on the roof and loosened another tile.

"That's no good!" said Mr Tiles. "That will cost you even more for another tile. Still, stamp about, Stamp-About. I don't mind you paying me more money!"

Stamp-About shouted, roared and stamped. Mr Tiles took no notice. He finished his work and went down the ladder. "Twenty one pounds!" he shouted to Stamp-About. "I'll get it from your sister as I'm sure you won't give it to me!"

Mr Stamp-About tried to get up from his chimney-pot seat, but he couldn't. Something seemed to be holding him back. What *could* it be?

"Come back! Don't you dare to ask my sister to pay you!" he yelled. "I'll pay you ten pounds and that's too much!"

"Goodbye," said Mr Tiles, jumping off the ladder. "Be careful you don't loosen any more tiles!"

He went into the house and told Stamp-About's sister she was to pay him twenty one pounds. She took it out of the cash box and gave it to him. He beamed and went out.

"Where's my brother?" called the sister. "I must just be certain the amount is right."

"He won't come in for a bit," said Mr Tiles with a grin. "You can ask him then."

Off he went, looking back now and again to see the furious Mr Stamp-About. There he sat on the chimney, trying his best to get up, but the glue was much too strong for him. He raged and stamped and shouted, and soon a collection of interested people came to watch.

"I'm stuck, I'm stuck!" he yelled. "Get me down!"

But people were afraid of his bad temper, and, besides, they were pleased to see horrid old Stamp-About stuck up on his own chimney-pot. And will you believe it, there he had to stay till a downpour of rain came and thinned out the glue.

Poor Mr Stamp-About. He was soaked through, and he missed his footing as he climbed down the roof, bounced down the ladder, and landed with a bump on the ground.

"Stamp-About! What *do* you think you are doing, sitting on a chimney-pot, shouting and yelling like that, and then falling off the roof?" cried his sister. "I'm ashamed of you. You can go straight up to bed. I've had enough of you today!"

And you'll hardly believe it, but Stamp-About had had such a lesson that he did go straight up to bed. He never forgot his day on the chimney-pot – and neither did anyone else!

Chinky takes a parcel

Chinky was doing his shopping in the pixie market. It was full today, and there were a great many people to talk to. Chinky was a chatterbox, so he loved talking.

His market bag was full. He had no more money to spend, and it was getting near his dinnertime. "I really must go home," said Chinky, and he picked up his bag.

"Hi," called Sally Simple, "did you say you were going home? Well, just deliver this parcel to Mrs Flip's next door to you, will you? It's for her party this afternoon."

"Certainly, Sally," said Chinky, and he took the square box, which felt very,

very cold indeed.

"You are sure you are going straight home?" asked Sally Simple anxiously. "I don't want you to take the parcel unless you are really off home now."

"I'm going this very minute," said Chinky. "Goodbye!"

He set off home – but he hadn't gone far before he met Dame Giggle, and she had a funny story to tell him. He listened and laughed, and then he thought of a *much* funnier story to tell Dame Giggle.

So it was quite ten minutes before he set off home again – and then who should he meet but Old Man Grumble, who stopped him and shook hands. Chinky hadn't seen Old Man Grumble for a long time, and he had a lot of news to tell him. He talked and he talked, and Old Man Grumble hadn't even time to get one grumble in!

"You *are* a chatterbox, Chinky," he said at last. "Goodbye, now! Perhaps you'll let me get a word in the conversation when next we meet."

Chinky set off again. The square cold parcel that he was carrying for Sally Simple seemed to have got very soft and squashy now. It was no longer cold either. It was rather warm and sticky!

"Goodness! I wonder what's in this parcel?" thought Chinky, hugging it under his arm.

A little drop of yellow juice ran out of one corner and dripped down Chinky's leg. It was ice-cream in the parcel – a big yellow brick of it, that Mrs Flip had ordered for her party. She meant to put it into her freezer when she got it, and then it would keep cold and icy till four o'clock.

Chinky went on his way, humming. Some more ice-cream melted and ran down his leg. Chinky didn't know. He was nodding excitedly at little Fairy Long-wings, who was standing at her gate.

"Hello, Long-wings!" called Chinky. "Glad to see you back. How did you enjoy your holiday?"

And, dear me, he stood talking at Long-wings' gate for ten minutes. Long-wings didn't tell him a word about her holiday, for Chinky was so busy chattering about himself and his garden and his shopping. And all the time the ice-cream dripped down his leg.

Well, when at last he arrived at Mrs Flip's the box was almost flat and empty. He handed it to Mrs Flip, and she looked at it in dismay.

"My ice-cream for the party!" she cried. "It's all melted! Look at your clothes, Chinky – what a mess they are in! Well, really, you might have brought it to me at once! I suppose Sally Simple gave it to you, thinking that you were coming straight home!"

"Well, so I did!" said Chinky indignantly. "I came *straight* home, as straight as could be!"

"I don't believe you," said Mrs Flip. "I know you, Chinky – the worst chatterbox in town! Oh yes! You met Mr So-and-so, and you talked to him for ages – and you saw Mrs This-and-that, and you chatted for ten minutes – and you came across Dame Such-and-such, and you had a good long talk! And all the time my ice-cream was melting. Take it! I don't want it now – it's just an empty box."

She threw it at Chinky, and it hit him on the nose. He was very angry. He shook his fist at Mrs Flip and shouted, "I shan't come to your party now! I just shan't come!"

"Well, don't then!" said Mrs Flip, and she went inside and banged her door. Chinky banged his.

Soon there was the sound of the ringing of a tricycle bell, and along came the ice-cream man. Mrs Flip heard him and out she ran. She bought the biggest ice-cream brick he had, all pink and yellow. She popped it into her freezer for the party that afternoon.

And when Chinky looked out of his

window at half-past four, he saw everyone busy eating ice-creams in Mrs Flip's garden, as happy as could be. Wasn't he cross!

"Why didn't I go straight home as I said I would? Why did I say I wouldn't go to the party? I talk too much, that's what's the matter with me!" said poor Chinky.

But chatterboxes can't be stopped — you try stopping one, and see!

Green-caps

Green-caps the goblin set up his little shop in the middle of the poppies. He loved their bright red flowers, and they in turn liked the merry little goblin who worked so hard in his tiny shop.

You can guess what Green-caps' work was. He made green hats for the little folk – nicely fitting little caps into which they could stick any coloured feather they liked. One by one the pixies, the brownies, the elves and the goblins came to him for a hat. He made them all neatly, and his stitches were so tiny that they could hardly be seen.

The poppies watched him sewing busily each day. They nodded their red heads and spoke together.

"We would like green caps, too."

"But what would be the sense of that?" asked Green-caps in surprise. "You could not wear my small green caps on your big red heads."

"We would like green caps for our *buds*," said the poppies, nodding in the wind. "You know, Goblin, when we are in bud, sometimes the winds are cold and they make us shiver. If we could wear green caps that fitted us well, we would be warm and cosy. We need not open our petals until the sun is really hot. The caps would keep us closed."

"But when you opened your pretty petals, the caps would look silly," said the goblin.

"We would throw them down to the ground as soon as we opened," said the poppies. "We shouldn't need them then. You could use them again, couldn't you, Green-caps?"

"Well – that's an idea," said the goblin. "I will make you some little caps for your buds and see if they will be of any use."

So Green-caps got busy and measured the buds for caps. He made some dear little round ones in green that fitted the buds tightly. He put one on each tiny bud.

"Now," he said to them, "when you feel that the sun is warm and you want to open and shake out your crumpled petals to dry, push hard at the cap – and it will split down the seams and fall off to the ground. Then I will come along and collect the pieces to make new caps."

The buds loved their green caps. They wore them as long as they needed warmth and protection – then they pushed them off so hard that they burst the seams – and the cap fell to the ground in pieces. Then the poppies shook out their silky red petals, and danced in the sun.

Green-caps came along, picked up the fallen pieces of cap, took them

home and sewed them neatly together again into another cap for a small bud.

Soon many little folk came to see the green caps he made for the poppies, because, as you can guess, the poppies talked about them to everyone. That meant a great deal more business for the goblin – and soon he was so busy that he had to send for more workers to help him. He still works among the poppies, as busy as can be, though he pops down a rabbit hole if you come near.

But though he hides himself, he can't hide the green caps he makes for the poppies! Go and have a look at them in the summer-time. You will find some poppies wearing them neatly, others just pushing them off, and still others with no caps at all, for they have burst the seams that Green-caps sewed – and the pieces are lying on the ground. If there are none on the ground you will know why – Green-caps has been there before you and picked them all up!

The pixies who forgot their corkscrew

Billy went out into the woods alone for the day. He was dreadfully worried. His daddy couldn't get any work to do, and there was no money coming in at all for food or clothes.

"You go and pick some berries," said his anxious mother. "Perhaps you can find enough for a pie, Billy."

So Billy took a basket, and went off for the day, wondering whether there was anything *he* could do to earn money. But he was a very little boy, and there didn't seem anything he could do at all. No one would let him drive a train, and he wasn't big enough to be a bus driver.

Billy's daddy was very clever, and

made knives, forks, corkscrews, hammers, pincers, and things like that. But it seemed as if nobody was ever going to want any more again; no orders came for any of those things, and the poor man couldn't sell enough to get money for food.

Billy thought of all this as he wandered about looking for berries. He could find very few, and before he had half-filled his basket he felt so hungry that he ate them all, and had to begin again.

"Here's a nice little path," he thought, as he saw a narrow way running between some very thick, tall trees. "I'll go along it and see if the berries grow any more thickly here."

He went down the path, looking for berries, and just as he came out into a wider path he saw a very strange sight.

Sitting on the ground in a ring, watching a basket being opened and unpacked, were a dozen little pixies, all very neat and proper. They looked hot, and when four little bottles of fizzy lemonade were taken out of the basket, they all clapped their hands.

"Good, good," they cried. "We are so thirsty!"

Billy stared in astonishment. Whatever were these tiny people, no bigger than dolls?

Soon a tablecloth was laid on the grass, no bigger than Billy's handkerchief, and pies and cakes and berries were arranged nicely on it. Every tiny pixie was given a plate and a glass, and soon they were quite ready to begin their meal.

Billy watched in excitement. It was the first time he had ever seen fairy-folk of any sort, and his heart beat quickly. What a story he would have to tell his father and mother when he got home!

"Can't we have a drink?" asked one of the pixies. "We're more thirsty than we are hungry."

So the bottles were taken up, and

then the chief pixie felt in his pockets for his corkscrew.

But it wasn't there! He felt in one pocket after another, and then turned to the waiting pixies.

"Will one of you lend me a corkscrew to draw the corks?" he asked. "I seem to have lost mine."

Each one felt in his pockets, but dear me, not a single pixie had thought of bringing a corkscrew with him! Every one of them had left it to someone else to bring!

"Oh dear, oh dear, oh dear!" they all cried in despair. "Here are lovely bottles of lemonade and we can't open them, and we're all *dreadfully* thirsty. Whatever shall we do?"

Then, because they were such tiny, excitable folk, they burst into tears, and wept into handkerchiefs as small as rose petals. Billy didn't like to see them doing that, and an idea came to him. He stepped forward, and spoke softly.

"Don't be frightened, little folk. I won't hurt you. I see your trouble, and if you can wait a while, I will go home and get my father to make you a corkscrew small enough to open your bottles."

The pixies jumped up in fright when he began to speak, but when they saw his kind face they ran to him, and listened eagerly.

"Kind boy, kind boy," they said. "Yes, fetch us a corkscrew, please!"

So Billy put his basket on the ground and ran as fast as he could until he reached home. Then he found his father, and begged him to make a tiny little corkscrew as quickly as he could.

"What nonsense is this?" asked his father grumpily. "Pixie folk, indeed! What rubbish, Billy! No, I'm not going to do such a silly thing. You're dreaming."

"No, indeed I'm not, Father," said Billy earnestly. "It's quite true. Anyway, Father, even if you don't

351

believe what I say, won't you make *me* a tiny little corkscrew, just to please me?"

So Billy's father got up and made him the tiniest little corkscrew you ever saw, so small that even a butterfly could easily pick it up. Billy thanked him and raced off with it. He found the pixies patiently waiting for him, and how they clapped their hands when they saw the little shining corkscrew!

"It would have taken us hours to go back for our corkscrew," they said. "Thank you, Billy. Now please do sit down and picnic with us. We can easily make our cakes and pies ten times bigger for you."

Well, Billy was hungry, so he sat down at once, and in two twinks one of the pies was a fine size, and he cut it and began to eat it. It was delicious. The chief pixie drew the corks with the tiny corkscrew, and soon everyone was eating and drinking merrily. Billy had never had such a jolly meal.

The pixies asked him about himself, and soon he had told them all about his father, and how he couldn't get work, and how worried his mother was.

"So she sent me out to get berries," said Billy. "But I couldn't find very many, and I was so hungry that I ate all I found!"

"We'll help you, in return for your kindness to us," cried the pixies, and after dinner they cleared away all the

bits, and then started out to look for berries. In an hour Billy's basket was so full that really it wouldn't hold another berry!

"Now I must go home," he said. "Goodbye, and thank you very much."

"Goodbye, and thank *you!*" shouted the pixies, and waved until Billy was out of sight.

Billy's mother was delighted with all the berries, and she made a lovely pie. "But goodness knows where our next meal is coming from!" she sighed. "Your poor father still hasn't any work to do."

Now the next day a very curious thing happened. People came running from everywhere around saying that they had lost their corkscrews, mislaid their pincers, forgotten where they had put their hammers, and I don't know what else. At first Billy's father was pleased, but soon he grew very much puzzled, for it did seem extraordinary that all the people should lose their things on exactly the same day!

He quickly sold the stock he had, and then had to set to work making some more. How hard he worked, and how delighted he was! He was a very good workman, and they all went away saying that they would certainly buy more things from him. So Billy's mother sighed with gladness, and hoped that better days were coming.

"It's the funniest, strangest, oddest thing I ever heard of, everyone losing just the things that I can make," said Billy's father that night. "I can't understand it. It's the biggest piece of luck I ever had!"

Billy smiled.

"Oh, Father, you didn't believe what I said yesterday about the pixies wanting a corkscrew for their lemonade," he said. "But they were very grateful, and I'm sure they have hidden away all these lost things so that people would come and buy yours."

"But they mustn't do that!" cried

Billy's mother. "The naughty little things! It's very kind of them, but they really mustn't go on doing that. They don't know wrong and right as we do. You must go and find them again tomorrow, Billy, and tell them not to do it any more."

So Billy went off next day to find the pixies, but search as he would, he couldn't see even one of them, though he felt sure they were somewhere near, peeping at him.

"If you're anywhere about, pixies, just listen a moment!" cried Billy at last. "You mustn't hide any more things, for though you mean it kindly, it is wrong! Goodbye, and thank you very much."

Trippit and the witch

Once upon a time, when Trippit the pixie was wandering through Hallo Wood, he met a witch.

Oh, what a witch she was! She wore a great high hat, as black as soot, with golden suns and silver stars stuck all over it, a cloak that was as red as fire, and earrings that reached to her shoulders and shone as brightly as diamonds. She had a hooked nose, slanting eyes, and a very nasty smile.

As soon as Trippit saw her he knew that he had met one of the most powerful witches in the world, and he wished to goodness that he had taken another path through the wood.

The witch stopped when she saw

Trippit, and took a sack off her back. Then she went up to him, caught hold of his collar, and popped him into the sack. She tied up the neck with string and flung the sack over her shoulder.

Trippit couldn't do anything. It wouldn't have been a bit of good running away even if he had had time. He just lay there in the sack and wondered what would happen to him.

The witch took him into her cottage in the very heart of the wood. She undid the sack and emptied Trippit out on the floor.

Now Trippit was a very smart and clever little creature, and he didn't mean to be turned into a cat to help the witch with her spells, or a frog or a mouse to be put into her magic cauldron and boiled up to make a very powerful magic spell. No – he'd wait his chance and see if he couldn't get the better of this hook-nosed witch.

"What are you going to do with me?" he asked.

"Wait and see," snapped the witch. "You can be my servant just for a few hours and tidy up my cottage."

"It *is* in a state!" said Trippit, looking round. "I wonder that a witch like you can't afford to have a good servant. You can't be much of a witch."

The witch boxed his ears, and told him to scrub the floor.

"I'm as powerful a witch as you'll ever see!" she said angrily.

"Oh, no, madam," said Trippit politely, looking for a scrubbing-brush and pail. "I've met many better witches than you, and I have seen the Wizard Do-a-lot perform some wonderful tricks. You couldn't do anything like him, I am sure."

"How dare you say things like that?" said the witch, pulling his hair hard. "I tell you, I'm the cleverest witch you'll ever see. Why, the things I do would hardly be believed!"

"I'm sure I shouldn't believe them if I heard of them," said Trippit, filling his pail with water. "I don't think you're much of a witch. I've never even heard of you!"

"What! Never heard of Witch Hoodle-hoo!" cried the old dame angrily. "Well, whatever is the world coming to?"

When Trippit heard her name, he trembled inside himself, for it was the name of one of the cleverest and worst witches in the world.

"It's bad luck to have been caught by her," he said to himself. "If ever I get out of this alive, I'll be lucky!"

"What other witches and wizards have you known?" asked Hoodle-hoo, quite amazed that this pixie didn't seem in the least afraid of her. He must be so used to living with powerful magicians and enchanters that he thought nothing of being caught by her. She couldn't hear how fast his heart was beating, or see how he trembled inside.

Trippit quickly made up some strange-sounding names.

"There was Wizard Popemmetopemme, who could turn himself into a blackbird and eat worms. There was the Enchanter Killomillotiddley-hi-ti, who could change into a roaring fire whenever he wanted to. There was the Magician Oonoloona-oh-my, who could turn into six different things at once."

"Pooh! I could do all those things *easily*!" said the witch scornfully. "They couldn't have been so clever if that was the best they could do."

"Well, there was one thing they could *not* do," said Trippit, beginning to scrub the floor hard.

"What was that?" asked the witch.

"Oh, never mind," said Trippit. "It's nothing *you* could do, anyway, so why bother about it?"

"Of course I could do it," said the witch impatiently. "Haven't I told you there is nothing I can't do? Tell me what this thing is that all those marvellous magicians couldn't do, and I'll soon show you how clever I am."

"No, I don't think I'll tell you," said Trippit, emptying away his dirty water and getting some fresh water. "You'd think you could do it, and then when you found you couldn't, you'd be angry with me and punish me."

"Tell me at once!" commanded the witch. "If you don't I'll sit you down in that pail of water."

"Well, if you put it like that," said Trippit, "I must tell you. None of those enchanters could turn into — what do you think? — a box of matches!"

"Well!" cried the witch in amazement. "An easy thing like that! I believe it's a trick you're playing on me, Pixie. I shan't turn into a box of matches."

"You couldn't if you tried!" said Trippit, rubbing the soap on the scrubbing brush. "I told you you couldn't."

"I say I'm not going to, because I think you'll play some nasty trick on me if I do," said the witch angrily.

"And I say you're not going to because you can't," said Trippit rudely.

The witch stared at him in such a bad temper that the hairs on her head bristled like a dog's. Trippit was very much afraid, but he didn't show it. He just went on scrubbing the floor.

"Well, I'll just turn myself into a box of matches this very minute," said the witch in a fierce tone, "and then, when I've changed back into a witch again I'll turn *you* into a box of matches and keep you on my mantelpiece to light my fires with!"

Trippit watched her. She took a thin golden wand and drew a circle around her where she stood. She shook some yellow powder over her head and then began to sing a strange magic song. As she sang she got smaller and smaller and smaller. Trippit watched in astonishment. He had never seen such a marvellous sight in his life.

When the witch was no bigger than an apple, she suddenly began to

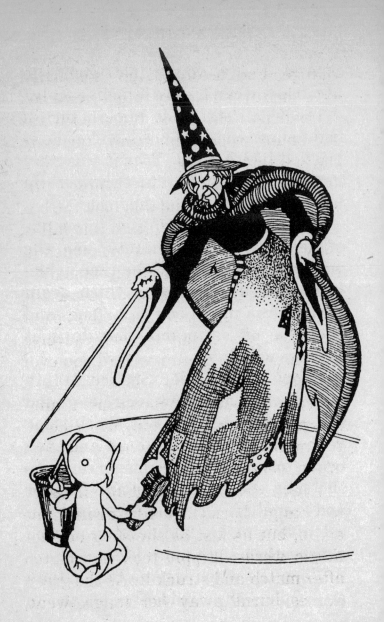

change, and before Trippit's startled eyes she turned slowly into a small box of matches. He knelt there with his scrubbing-brush in his hand, staring in the greatest surprise.

Then, quick as lightning, he stretched out his hand and took the box of matches. He opened it. It was full of matches. He took one out and struck it. It burned with a fierce green flame.

"I have done as you said," came the witch's voice suddenly from the box of matches. "Am I not clever? Cleverer than any enchanter or wizard you ever knew?"

"Yes, but not so clever as I am," laughed Trippit. "I'm going to strike all the matches, and that will be the end of you, dear witch!"

With a scream the witch began to try to change back into her own shape again, but as fast as she sang out her magic words Trippit took out match after match and struck it. As the green flames burnt away her magic went, and at last she had none left to change herself back into her right shape.

"I played you a fine trick, didn't I?" said Trippit, laughing. "Well, well, you'll not be wanting this cottage any more, will you? So I may as well take it for myself. And you said, didn't you, that you'd turn me into a box of matches and keep me on the mantelpiece? So I'll keep *you* there instead! Now, you be good, or there's no knowing what I might do with an empty matchbox!"

He popped the box up on the mantelpiece, and there it is to this day, for he still lives in Hoodle-hoo's hidden-away cottage in the heart of Hallo Wood. And when his friends hear the story of how he tricked the witch, they are most astonished.

They look at the empty matchbox up on the mantelpiece, and they don't touch it. They are afraid it might turn back into a wicked witch again. But it never will!

Black boot buttons

One day Betty and Fred had such a funny adventure. They were going home from school over the fields when they heard someone saying something over and over again.

"Oh dear, oh dear, oh dear, oh dear, oh dear!" said somebody. And then he started off again. "Oh dear, oh dear, oh dear, oh dear, oh dear!"

"Whoever can that be?" wondered Betty. "It's someone on the other side of the hedge, Fred. Let's look, shall we?"

So they squeezed through a hole in the hedge and looked. And on the other side they saw a strange sight.

A small man sat in the grass. He had on a tall, pointed hat set with little bells. He wore a green tunic and long black stockings, and on his legs were high button boots – with no buttons on! The children stared in surprise.

"Oh dear, oh dear, oh dear, oh dear, oh dear!" began the little man again – and then he caught sight of the children.

"Oh dear, oh . . ." he began, but Betty stopped him.

"Please don't say it again or we shall laugh!" she said. "What's the matter?"

"Look at my boots," said the little man. "I was on my way to visit my brother, Sir Up-and-down, who lives in

the wood yonder, in a very nice oak tree. I sat down here to rest a little and fell asleep. When I awoke I found that a mischievous pixie had been along and cut all the buttons off my button boots. He has taken them with him too — and now here am I, on my way to visit Sir Up-and-down, and haven't even a button on my boots!"

The children stared. They knew they must be talking to someone belonging to the fairies. But he didn't look like a fairy. He was very upset about his boots.

"Oh dear, oh dear, oh dear, oh . . ." he began again, and Betty and Fred laughed. It did sound so funny.

"Don't laugh. It's rude," said the little man crossly. "You should help people when they are in trouble, not laugh at them."

"Well, we would like to help you," said Betty. "But I don't see how we can. We don't wear button boots or shoes, only laced ones. We have no buttons to give you, and the village shop is two miles away. It would take too long to go there and back. Besides, today is early closing day."

"Just my luck," said the little man gloomily. "If only I could find some buttons. I could put them on in a trice then go to visit my brother."

He got up and looked down at his boots. He shook his head and began to walk off slowly. "Oh dear, oh dear, oh dear, oh dear, oh dear!" the children heard him say as he went.

They watched him go, and then they turned to walk home. They felt excited to have met such a strange little man, who had a brother with such a funny name, living in such a strange place.

Now as they went on their way they came to a thick ivy hedge – and on it, growing in big clusters, were berries as round and as black as boot buttons. Fred saw them first and stopped with a shout.

"Betty, look! The ivy has berries just

like boot buttons. Do you suppose they would do for the little man? If he belongs to the fairies he may know some magic and could sew them on his boots quite easily."

"Let's run back and tell him," said Betty.

So the two children ran back down the path, calling loudly, "Little man, little man, stop!"

The little fellow had not gone very far. He stopped and ran back to the children.

"What is it?" he cried. "Have you got some black boot buttons for me?"

"Yes," said Betty. "Come and look!"

She led him to the ivy hedge, and the little man gazed at the clusters of black berries there.

"The very thing," he said. "Pick me some, please."

Betty and Fred picked him a big bunch. He took the biggest and blackest berries, doubled the stalks of each one over to make a loop, and took a needle and cotton from a case in his pocket.

He sat down. He muttered a magic word to the needle, and to the children's great astonishment it began to sew on those ivy buttons as quick as could be. In half a minute the little man's boots had a row of buttons on each one. He buttoned them up and beamed at the children.

"Just the very thing," he said. "Why didn't I think of it myself? Thank you, children. Is there anything I can do for you in return?"

"Do you think you could manage to let us have a kitten of our own?" asked Betty in excitement. "We've always wanted one, but we've never had one."

"Oh yes, I'll manage that easily," said the little man. "Look on your doorstep tomorrow morning. Goodbye now, I'm off to see my brother."

He ran off and the children went home in great excitement – and will you believe it, when they opened the door next morning there on the doorstep they found a dear little kitten, with fur as black as the ivy berries! They called it Ivy, of course, and it still lives with them, though now it has grown into an enormous black cat with green eyes. Betty is sure it came from a witch.

Would you like to see some of the black boot buttons that the little man sewed on to his boots? Then go and look at the berries on the ivy in spring, and you will see some. They are round and black – just like boot buttons!

The ball that vanished

Jenny and Fred had a beautiful big rubber ball. It was bright blue one side and bright red the other side, and when it rolled along quickly it wasn't blue or red, but purple instead.

"It goes purple when it rolls because the blue and the red mix up together and make purple!" said Jenny, who knew quite a lot about painting.

They played every day with the big blue and red ball. They rolled it, they kicked it, they threw it, they bounced it. It didn't mind a bit what they did with it. It just loved everything.

And then one day it vanished. It really was rather extraordinary, because neither Jenny nor Fred saw where it went.

They were having a fine game of 'Throwing-the-ball-over-the-house'. I don't know whether you have ever played that game, but if your house isn't too high it is rather fun. One of you stands at the front of the house, and the other one stands at the back, and you can only do it if Mother says you may. Anyway, Mother said that Fred and Jenny might play it till dinner time.

So Fred stood at the back and Jenny stood at the front. Fred threw the ball high into the air and it went right over the house. Jenny saw it coming over the chimneys and she gave a shout of joy. She held out her hands for it, and it dived right down into them.

"I've caught it, Fred!" she cried. "Look out – it's coming back to you!"

She threw it up into the air – but she didn't throw it hard enough, and it struck the tiles, rolled down the roof, and fell back into her hands again. She threw it once more, and this time it sailed right over the top. Fred gave a shout.

"I see it! It's coming! Good throw, Jenny. I've caught it!"

Then Fred aimed the ball high again and up it went over the house once more. But Jenny didn't call out that it was coming. There was no sound from her at all.

"Jenny! Have you caught it?" shouted Fred.

"No. It hasn't come yet," said Jenny, puzzled. "Did you throw it? Did it go right over the roof?"

"Of course," said Fred. "Didn't you hear me shout? It *must* have fallen on your side, Jenny. Look for it."

So Jenny looked all over the front garden, but not a sign of that big blue and red ball did she see. It was most annoying. Fred came running round to the front.

"Haven't you found it yet?" he asked. "Jenny, you don't know how to look!"

"I *do*!" said Jenny crossly. "I've looked everywhere. It's you that doesn't know how to *throw*! The ball must have fallen back into your half of the garden. I shall go and look there!"

So Fred hunted in the front garden and Jenny hunted in the back one. But neither of them could find that ball. It really had completely vanished. It was very odd.

They went in and told Mother. "Could a ball disappear into the air?" asked Fred.

"Of course not," said Mother. "It's a pity if you have lost that nice ball. It really was a beauty."

Well, that wasn't the only unpleasant thing to happen that day. When the children went into their room to look for another toy to play with, they found the room full of smoke.

"Mother, Mother, the house is on fire!" said silly Jenny, with a scream. But Fred knew better.

"It's the chimney smoking!" he cried. "Mother, come and put the fire out in the grate. The smoke is coming out into the room."

Mother hurried in, vexed and worried. How she did hate to see all the smoke pouring out and making things black and dirty!

"I can't imagine why it is doing this," she said, vexed. "The sweep only came a few weeks ago, and usually this chimney goes at least six months without cleaning. Oh, dear – it's no good. I must ring up the sweep and tell him to come. Some damp soot must have stopped up the chimney."

So the sweep came with his brushes, and the children watched him in delight. Sweeping a chimney seemed a most glorious thing to do, and both Jenny and Fred made up their minds that when they were grown up they would be chimney-sweeps.

The sweep put a brush up the chimney, and then fitted another pole to the brush handle. He pushed that up the chimney too. Then he fitted on another pole and pushed that up as well.

"You see, Jenny, all these long poles push the brush higher and higher up the chimney, sweeping as it goes, till it comes to the top!" said Fred in delight.

"Does the brush come right out of the top of the chimney?" asked Jenny.

"Of course," said the sweep, his black face smiling at them, showing very white teeth. "You run outside into the garden, Missy, and shout to me when you see my old black brush poking itself out of the top of your chimney! Then I'll know it is right out and I won't fit on any more poles!"

So out went Fred and Jenny and watched the chimney. And soon Jenny gave a scream of joy.

"Look, Fred, look! The brush is just coming out!"

Sure enough, something was coming out of the chimney. It was the sweep's brush – but on top of it was something round and black and strange. Whatever could it be?

"What's that on top of the brush?" said Fred. "Is it a black stone, do you think? I'll go and tell the sweep."

So into the house he ran and told the surprised sweep that there was something on top of his brush.

"A bird's nest, maybe," said the sweep. "Birds sometimes build their nests in a chimney, you know, and that stops it up and makes it smoke. I'll come and look."

So the sweep left his long poles standing upright in the grate, and went out to look. He stared and stared at the thing on top of his round brush, and then he went back indoors again.

"I'll shake and wriggle my poles so that the brush throws off that thing, whatever it is," he said. "I really don't know *what* it can be."

So he shook his poles and the brush shook too – and off came that round

black thing, bounced all the way down the roof and fell into the garden!

And it was – yes – you've guessed right! It was the children's big ball, very black, very sooty, and very sorry for itself indeed!

"Oh! It's our ball!" shouted Fred, picking it up and making his hands all sooty. "Oh, Jenny – it fell down the chimney when I threw it up! And it stopped up the chimney and made it smoke! It must just have fitted the chimney-pot!"

Jenny was excited and pleased. "Let's wash it," she said. "Won't Mother be surprised!"

So they washed the ball, and it came all clean and blue and red again. But it never bounced quite so high as it once used to, because the chimney had been hot, and the ball had been nearly cooked.

And now the children don't like to play 'Throw-the-ball-over-the-house' in case it pops down a chimney again! Mother says it really costs her too much to look after a ball that is so fond of chimneys.